The last tunnel emptied into a portal, beyond which spun a drum painted black and white, its swirling colors creating a hypnotic effect. Getting through it would be tricky but not awfully difficult. Suave stood on the portal beside Alina, crowding her in an area meant for smaller bodies.

"Think you can handle that?" she asked.

"That's kid stuff."

"I'm dizzy just looking at it."

He conceded. "My turn to help you."

Suave grasped her forearm, leading her into the final part of the maze. Then things went downhill after the first step, with both of them losing their footing. Alina fell first. Suave struggled against the laws of physics and lost, falling on top of her.

It was a tangle of arms and legs, and they ended up in a compromising position with one on top of the other. Alina yelped and laughed, grabbing Suave's shoulders and saving his glasses before they slipped from his face. Her hand brushed against his cheek, and she felt the heat of his skin on her fingertips.

She saw black and white and the color red from somewhere—a fiery, vibrant red—and the brilliant blue of his eyes, much too close to hers. His mouth was moist, ripe for a kiss. *One kiss, from a man's mouth.* As he fought to help balance her, she leaned closer to him, reveling in the sinfully wonderful taste of his kiss. . . . .

BOOK YOUR PLACE ON OUR WEBSITE AND MAKE THE READING CONNECTION!

We've created a customized website just for our very special readers, where you can get the inside scoop on everything that's going on with Zebra, Pinnacle and Kensington books.

When you come online, you'll have the exciting opportunity to:

- View covers of upcoming books

- Read sample chapters

- Learn about our future publishing schedule (listed by publication month *and author*)

- Find out when your favorite authors will be visiting a city near you

- Search for and order backlist books from our online catalog

- Check out author bios and background information

- Send e-mail to your favorite authors

- Meet the Kensington staff online

- Join us in weekly chats with authors, readers and other guests

- Get writing guidelines

- AND MUCH MORE!

**Visit our website at
http://www.pinnaclebooks.com**

IN YOUR ARMS

Consuelo Vazquez

PINNACLE BOOKS
Kensington Publishing Corp.
http://www.encantoromance.com

PINNACLE BOOKS are published by

Kensington Publishing Corp.
850 Third Avenue
New York, NY 10022

All Kensington Titles, Imprints, and Distributed Lines are available at special quantity discounts for bulk purchases for sales promotions, premiums, fund-raising, and educational or institutional use. Special book excerpts or customized printings can also be created to fit specific needs. For details, write or phone the office of the Kensington special sales manager: Kensington Publishing Corp., 850 Third Avenue, New York, NY 10022, attn: Special Sales Department, Phone: 1-800-221-2647.

Pinnacle and the P logo, Encanto and the E logo Reg. U.S. Pat. & TM Off.

First Printing: June 2001
10 9 8 7 6 5 4 3 2 1

Printed in the United States of America

Prologue

Brendan Rivera wasn't a particularly religious man, but he hadn't stopped praying since right before he entered the hospital OR. That must be the way it was for guys who suddenly found themselves on a sinking ship or overpowered on the battlefield or worse—at the mercy of a brand-new human being.

He guessed it was all pretty similar. The silent prayer that said, *Oh, God, please let me get through this in one piece!*

"How are you doing, baby?"

The voice, sweet even in its raspiness, prompted him to turn his head. Good timing, too. One of the two obstetricians was brandishing the scalpel in the air, preparing for the first incision.

"Hey, I'm . . . I'm okay. You're the star here, honey." He gave his young fiancée's hand a comforting squeeze. "How are you doing, Tracy?"

"Great. My nose is stopped up, and I feel like I'm going to toss my cookies any minute now. Other than that, I'm up to taking a drive out to the desert tonight. And you?"

"Sure. *You* can drive."

One of the two doctors, a stocky associate of Dr. Mahmoud's, found the suggestion pleasantly amusing. Tracy knew that she wasn't going anywhere that evening. Especially not with the baby, who was making his or her debut into the world a week and a half earlier than expected.

Dr. Mahmoud had patiently explained everything to both of them, such as why the emergency caesarean had to be performed: to prevent the expectant mother from more hours of arduous labor and to prevent the baby from going into distress. After exhausting and stressful hours of labor, Tracy reluctantly agreed to forego giving birth naturally. Suave didn't know what was more frightening: watching her go through more excruciating pain and discomfort, or witnessing her going under the knife.

Throughout the impromptu discussion, Dr. Mahmoud's voice remained steady and confident. Between the obstetrician's gentle assurances and the epidural that finally numbed her from the waist down, Tracy was holding up well. She was a real trooper.

Brendan—or Suave, as he was known to his family and friends—was falling apart at the seams. He wouldn't reveal his fear to Tracy, and he forced his hands to stay steady. Luckily, he was only shaking inside.

"You're doing very well there, Mr. Rivera," Dr. Mahmoud said heartily, making everyone laugh, including Tracy. "You might want to look away for the next, oh . . . half hour or so."

"Look away?" Suave sounded incredulous. He

regarded Tracy. "You're watching this, aren't you?"

She glanced away from the domed mirrors hanging overhead, which gave her a view of the doctor's hands, covered by surgical gloves streaked with blood, and her swollen belly. Tracy was all baby; the rest of her build as thin and slight as it was before the pregnancy. She never looked smaller or more delicate to Suave, and she stirred his protective instincts.

"Yep. Every second of it, Suavecito."

"Good, baby. So am I."

Dr. Mahmoud broke the moment's romance by warning, "Just move back and away from Tracy and the table, young man, if you think you're going to pass out. We'll take care of you later."

Behind the surgical mask, Suave opened his mouth to protest, then closed it abruptly. So the doctor thought him a typical, macho dad-to-be, who didn't know he couldn't handle the sight of a little blood? Or was it that Dr. Mahmoud saw him as a nineteen-year-old kid, suddenly thrust into a role he couldn't handle—as an expectant father?

He could only thank himself for giving the doctor that impression. Throughout the last two months of Tracy's difficult pregnancy, hadn't he roughed it through a few of those "sympathy pains"? He'd felt queasy some mornings, in addition to a little aching throb in the small of his back now and then, just like his bride-to-be. He'd joined her in those midnight cravings for pineapple sundaes and had even gained some weight.

Tracy found it adorable, and the doctor had

been amused. Yet, they'd made it through that time. And this was graduation day.

Please, God, let this baby be all right.

Yes, there was blood. Blood on the sheets, blood on the doctors' hands, all the way up to their forearms. Surprisingly, Suave wasn't dizzy or reeling with nausea. His stomach and throat tightened, and he couldn't move a muscle in his body, but his fascination overcame everything else.

The doctor actually reached his hands fully into the womb. In a matter of seconds, the baby's head was visible through the open incision, more fragile than fine china, covered by amniotic fluid, blood, and soft tresses of light brown hair.

Suave's gaze shot over to Tracy, who let out a cooing sort of laugh at the view afforded her by the mirrors above them. He drew closer to her, enveloping her hand in both of his.

They were both so far now from that awful afternoon, when she had called him from Nevada. The call came as a shock to him, since he'd heard through friends that she'd eloped with someone she'd met and then moved across the country. He'd begun accepting that it was over, that his hope to be with her had run out. He thought he'd never see her again—and then came the call. He had hardly understood what she was saying, her plea garbled between crying and hiccups.

He left me. He left me, and I'm pregnant. Suave, if you could just come here. Please, come. I don't wanna have this baby alone.

He snapped back to the present.

Swiftly and gently, the obstetrician freed the

rest of the tiny baby from the womb. Suave's eyes widened in utter amazement at the sight of little pink fists punching at the air.

Dr. Mahmoud nodded, jubilantly announcing, "It's a girl! It's a girl, and she is a beauty!"

Cheers rose up from the attending nurses, the pediatrician, and the anesthesiologist.

"Oh, my God, Suave, you were right!" Tracy was tickled. "You said it was going to be a little girl!"

"Ahhh, that was a lucky guess, baby." He shrugged. "I didn't care what it was. Boy, girl. Just somebody to love, right? That and she's healthy."

The baby girl gave an indignant little cry. Suave marveled at her lovely voice, certain he would never forget the first time he heard it. Dr. Chibbaro, a slender woman of Mexican descent, had the baby cleaned up and wrapped, almost like a present, in a teal-and-white hospital blanket. She turned to him with her arms slightly stretched out, offering him the baby.

"Quieres cargar tu hija, Papi?" she asked, the corners of her eyes crinkled with a smile even under her mask.

Momentarily, Suave froze. His stare dropped from the pediatrician's face to the precious parcel in her arms, already drowsy with sleep induced by the mother's anesthesia. It wasn't so much fear as a bittersweet feeling in his chest that prevented him from moving faster to take the baby in his arms.

Would you like to hold your daughter, Daddy? Suave repeated silently.

"That's fine. Support her neck. That's good,"

Dr. Chibbaro encouraged him, as she fitted the child snugly into his arms.

Turning to his side, he held the baby at an angle for Tracy to see. In her sleep, the little girl scrunched her mouth and brow in a pout. She wasn't a doll or a plaything, but rather a mountain of responsibility, a real soul encased within a small, helpless body. Someone who was going to need to be looked after, who was going to minimize her parents' sleep for quite a while, who would depend entirely upon them. From that day forward, their lives would never be the same again.

And she was another man's baby. Someone Tracy's former husband had decided that he could live without, like her beautiful mother. He had abandoned them both.

Wiping the tears from her face with the back of her hands, Tracy turned her head to them. "Isn't she gorgeous, Suave? What do you think?"

He'd promised to take care of her and her child. Maybe he hadn't really understood what he was getting himself into, Sure, he could work and put a roof over their heads and stock a refrigerator with food. He'd dropped out of school to join her in Vegas, and he'd found a job soon enough, working in the maintenance department at one of the hotels. It would be hard, but they'd get by.

What troubled him was a crazy, unfounded thought that the baby wouldn't accept him. That there'd come a day when she refused to call him Papi or Daddy, flatly informing him that he wasn't her real father. He knew without a doubt that after raising her as his own and giving her his love, she'd still break his heart.

And why was he allowing that ridiculous scenario, so far into the future, to ruin what had to be the most breathtaking afternoon of his life?

"I think she's beautiful, Trace. And I think we make a real nice family."

"So do I. You're going to be a great father, Suave." Her voice fell to a whisper. "You're the one I should've married in the first place. Forgive me."

"No, *vaya*. There's nothing to forgive, baby. I'm gonna love both my girls so much."

"You'd better, because we're not going to let you go!"

She stroked the baby's side, then softly ran her hand down Suave's cheek. He hadn't noticed his own tears, streaming down his face.

Dr. Mahmoud waved at them hesitantly. "I'm sorry to break this up, but we have to take care of the little one and her mother. You may step out for a few minutes, young man. Very good job."

"Yeah, thanks. You did good, too, Doctor," Suave said, laughing with the nurses. He placed the baby back into the pediatrician's arms and bent to kiss Tracy's forehead through his mask before leaving the room.

Tracy loved him. He was secure in that fact, that she loved him deeply. As far back as high school, where they'd first met, he'd meant something to her.

Yet there was a difference between loving someone and being *in love* with someone. For Suave, those two things were one and the same when it came to Tracy. He didn't care what anyone said, whether it was his parents telling him that he was making a mistake by throwing away his future on "that girl," or his best friend, Tamara Romero, who'd admitted more than once that she couldn't comprehend what he saw in Tracy.

He loved her, and he was in love with her, and he couldn't imagine giving that love to anyone else. Even though he knew he belonged to the little honey in the hospital's nursery the moment he held her in his arms.

After returning his surgical garb, he stepped out of the building to catch a breath of fresh air. The Nevada air was hot and arid, sweeping in from the vacant field behind the parking lot.

He was now a father. *What a rush!* He suspected that he should've been more afraid than he was— and the fear was there, that was true. But there was also a joy that was impossible to describe, and he embraced it with excitement.

In time, Tracy would fall in love with him. It was bound to happen. She'd accepted his proposal, agreeing to be married shortly after the baby's birth, and she'd keep her maiden name.

Ellie would have his name. He and Tracy had tossed around names until they mutually decided upon "Antonio" for a boy or "Ellie" for a girl.

In time, they'd become a family. Maybe he'd return to school and earn his degree in business administration, and they'd buy a house right there in Nevada. In time, his wife would fall as head-over-heels in love with him as he was with her, and the little girl would love him as the only father she'd ever known.

Time. The very thing that would be taken from them eventually, altering the dreams Suave had for his family of three.

One

The house was nothing like the old place down in Miami. Vacated by the previous owners, an older couple who moved to a senior community further down the New Jersey coast, it was about seventy or eighty years old. There was not a stick of furniture in it and the wallpaper was ancient. It was empty and more than a little lonely.

Its exterior was uninspired, to put it kindly. The brickface could've used a cosmetic makeover, and the same went for the kitchen and bathroom—although the latter had an old, quaint personality to it. Old and quaint was "in." The real estate agent, a man who looked like he'd dip into the cooking wine when the beer was all gone, touted the place's main assets.

The price was dirt cheap, the exact description of Alina Romero's house-buying budget. For the money, the prospective owner found herself with a master bedroom and two smaller ones, a fair-sized backyard choked with weeds, and a short walk to the boardwalk and beach. So, the house did have its merits and possibilities.

Sort of.

Tamara Romero, Alina's younger sister, inspected the master bedroom's closet and found more wire hangers than a family could use in a lifetime, along with some objects she didn't quite recognize.

"Eh, say, those come with the house," Arnold Peterson, the not-so-savvy agent, announced confidently.

"What comes with the house?" Mercedes, the baby of the family, peered into the closet over her sister's shoulder.

"The hangers. Those mothballs, too."

"Oh! So *that's* what those things are!" Tamara closed the closet door. "How lovely!"

Sensing a sale slipping through his fingers, Peterson blurted, "Really nice neighborhood, you know? Got a park and a ShopRite about a quarter of a mile from here."

"Hmmm. How far are we from a Home Depot?" Alina asked sweetly.

"Home Depot? Oh, not far at all! That's maybe another half mile down the highway."

"Good. That should be helpful."

"The school bus stops right down at the corner. School's a few blocks from here, close by. Great school system!"

"I hope so. I'll be working in it, come September."

The man's bloodshot eyes bulged. "That's right. You're a teacher. Where are you—"

"Harry Truman Elementary. I'll be taking over a fourth-grade class."

"Harry Truman Elem—well, *that's the same school!*" Peterson flailed his arms in the air. "It's destiny! You and this house were meant to be together, Mrs. Oceguera!"

"Yeah, it sure is starting to look that way." She waved her hand in the direction of the hallway. "I'm just going to have another look at the dining room, if you don't mind."

"Not at all, *señora*. Look to your heart's content." Turning his attention to a small, brown leather notebook in his hands, Peterson scribbled something on a page with heavy, loud strokes of his pen.

Whatever is he writing in there? Alina wondered as she walked back down the stairwell. *Teacher plus proximity to school equals my commission on a house that's been on the market for two years.* Or he could've been paraphrasing P.T. Barnum: *There's a sucker born every minute, and at long last, I've reeled one of those babies in.*

"And it's desperation, Mr. Peterson," she whispered to herself, entering the dining room through the Mediterranean doorway, which she had to admit appealed to her. "Not destiny."

The house wasn't all that bad. She'd had a dining area in her house in Florida, sectioned off between the living room and kitchen. This was a dining *room*, not terribly impressive in size but with enough space for her cherrywood table and matching china cabinet, which were now in a rented storage space. And the room boasted two huge windows, through which the afternoon sun cast abundant golden light.

She sank down onto the dusty, mustard-colored carpet and sat, hugging her arms around her knees. It wasn't the impetuous desire to look at the dining room again that had brought her down there, but rather the need for a few moments of solitude.

The last time she'd gone house-hunting, she'd been accompanied by her husband. She and Marco had toured three houses, at the most, before settling on the last one as their starter home. With two bedrooms and an aboveground swimming pool, it would suit them perfectly until they could build their dream home later on.

Those were the plans and dreams that would now never materialize. She'd accepted that . . . finally. Still, the whole situation was so strange, selling that precious home she'd shared with Marco and their son and beginning the process all over again, this time with her sisters.

Not that she didn't appreciate the gesture. Tamara had taken time off from work, and Mercedes had driven down from upstate New York to accompany her. Her sisters and parents were the reason she'd moved back to New Jersey—that, and the importance of her son's relationship with his grandparents and aunts and uncles.

There was something about family that couldn't be duplicated. Being around her sisters again, she'd already overcome the feeling of being alone.

Footsteps resounded on the stairs. She remained seated comfortably on the floor.

Eagerly, Peterson charged full-steam ahead, reiterating, "Reeeeeally convenient, being so close to that beach! In the summer, you pack a cooler and some towels, and you're good to go!"

"That's wonderful," Alina murmured, lost in her own thoughts.

"So, are you ready to go back to the office? I'll put that bid in for you in a jiffy. Tonight. I'll drive it down to the sellers tonight."

Mercedes glanced warily at Alina, and Tamara came to her aid.

"That's very kind of you, Mr. Peterson," she said softly, "I think my sister might want to take some time to think it over."

Instantly, the agent looked crestfallen. "What's—what's to think over? It's a steal at this price. Sure, I know it's not much now, but the place has great potential."

Alina cleared her throat. "Would you mind giving us a few minutes, Mr. Peterson?"

"No. No, uh. . . ." Moping, he shrugged. "Go right ahead, ladies. I'll be, eh, outside on the porch. If you need me, holler."

As soon as he was gone, Mercedes sat on the floor beside Alina. With that same dulcet affection of the little girl who Alina remembered, she hugged Alina's neck and kissed her on the cheek.

"I love seeing you and Justin again, so much," she said.

"It's mutual, Mercy. And Justin loves his Uncle Quinn."

Tamara, ever the businesswoman, brought them back onto the subject at hand as she slowly paced the floor.

"Don't let this guy pressure you, Alina," she advised. "And don't marry yourself to a house that quickly."

"Yes, I've been hearing you say those same words for about seven houses already." Alina subdued her exasperation. "Justin and I can't go on living in Mami and Papi's basement forever, Tammy."

"It's really not a bad house, you know?" Mercedes pitched in. "And that mortgage wouldn't drain the life out of you, either."

Alina was about to agree. Then Tamara asked, "And why do you think it's such a bargain? This is what you'd call a handyman's special."

Mercedes countered her. "So?"

"So? You know a handyman?"

"It so happens that I know *two.*"

"You do, huh?"

"Yeah. Quinn and Diego! I'll volunteer my husband; you volunteer yours."

"No, no, that's out." Alina shook her head vehemently. "I'm not imposing on anyone. I'll manage this myself. Somehow."

Tamara frowned. "You sound like you've already made the decision to buy this place."

"I think I should go for it, Tammy. I don't know." She tossed locks of her long, rich brown hair over her shoulder. "I don't want to keep living in my parents' house. I'm an adult."

"That's debatable," Mercedes teased.

There was a pause. Tamara glanced out the window, sighing. "It's just that I don't want to see you make any snap decisions. I mean, this house could turn out to be a money pit."

"That's why I need to hire an inspector to check out the property," Alina reminded her. "So he can warn me about the flood damage and the termites before I'm sitting in water and nibbled-up wood."

"True. But there's one thing an inspector can't tell you. And that is," Mercedes said, "Do you *like* the house? Can you see yourself happy here?"

Alina rested her head against the wall. "Do I like it as much as the old place? No. That was home. But, can we be happy here?"

She stopped as soon as her throat started clenching. There were no memories in this old house, sweet and sad as they were. No reminders of her husband, whose life had ended without any warning whatsoever. She tugged at some frayed threads on the hem of her jeans.

Then she continued. "I think so. In time. Justin would love having his own room again. And I could put that third bedroom to good use, too. I should put the bid in tonight."

Tamara crouched down, joining them on the floor.

"Alina, it hasn't sold in two years. Be a little suspicious, at least." She smiled. "You, who are always so trusting! Sleep on it. Call Mr. Peterson. Tell him you'd like to see it one more time. And bring someone with you."

"I already did. That's why you two are here."

"No. Bring a *man,*" Tamara specified. "Peterson's the type of guy that, even if a woman's an engineer, he assumes all she's thinking about is which color scheme would look best in the living room. You have a man there, barking questions at him left and right, and I guarantee the guy's coming up with something better than 'the mothballs come with the house.' "

Mercedes tittered. "I'll find out if Quinn can make it down here sometime this week."

"Why? We live a lot closer. Diego wouldn't mind accompanying you, Alina."

She warmed to the idea. "Okay. I'll wait then and come back—but at Diego's convenience."

"All right, then. Let's go break the news to Hanger Man!" Mercedes rose and helped Alina to her feet and then walked beside her to the front door. "You know what you need, girl? Some time to yourself."

"I'm a mother. Mothers don't get time to themselves."

"Now that's an encouraging thing to say to a woman who wants to join the ranks of motherhood." Mercedes laughed. "You've been through a lot this year, Alina. What's one little weekend?"

Temptation nagged at her. So far, the past year had been anything but a picnic. Between selling the house in Miami, moving back to the state she'd grown up in, and finding a suitable home at reasonable price, Alina's nerves were on edge.

Between temporarily living in her parents'

basement apartment, which made decent but cramped living quarters for her and her toddler son, and working in a new school in the fall, the stress was mounting.

"Quinn and I could watch Justin for you. It'd give him a good idea of what to expect, if a pregnancy test says yes, after all."

"That could backfire, you know."

"No, come on. But back to you. Mami and Papi hardly ever use that house by the lake. Tamara and I are up there with the guys more than they are. I'll loan you my key, if you want."

"I have to think about it, Mercy. I have a lot to think about."

Having joined her sisters for breakfast that morning before meeting the real estate agent, Alina wanted to get back to Justin. At that very second, their father, Alejandro Romero, was engaged in his favorite pastime—spoiling his only grandson. Hopefully, both her sisters would announce their own blessed event that year. That would rightfully divide their parents' spoiling techniques among the kids, or they would go bankrupt in the process.

She left behind a disheartened Arnold Peterson, who seemed ready to drive his car off a pier at the postponement of the sale, and drove her secondhand Nissan to the highway. She drove slowly, taking time to notice the surroundings, which were only now becoming familiar to her again.

The South Jersey community truly wasn't a bad little town. Most of the homes were either brick or Victorian, and the majority of the shops were located on Main Street. The fragrance of sea salt scented the wind coursing through the car's open windows. A row of larger Victorians—bed and breakfasts—lined the streets facing the boardwalk. Farther down was the town's main claim to fame: the Church of Christ, Resurrected, established in 1872, the year the town was founded.

She'd returned to a year of four seasons. Alina had missed that, living in Florida's never-ending summer. The proximity to her job couldn't be beat, either. As she passed the park, where four teenage boys were enjoying an energetic game of basketball, she thought about her son. Horizon Beach appeared to be a good enough place as any for Justin to someday call his hometown.

Maybe another tour of the prospective homestead with her brother-in-law, Diego Santamaria, would help her make a solid decision. By now, she was accustomed to being the sole decision-maker in the family—a responsibility thrust upon her three years earlier when Marco died.

But just because she was used to it didn't mean that it ever got any easier.

The beauty across the room was Alina Romero. Suave was certain of it.

Except that she wasn't a Romero anymore. Her last name was something else now since she'd married that good-looking, popular ballplayer in school and moved down to Florida. But Tamara, who'd recently renewed her longtime friendship with him, would have adamantly disagreed.

Once a Romero, always a Romero.

"Daddy, watch out!"

"What?" He spun around in time to get bopped in the chest by a Ping-Pong ball.

"Oops!" His daughter, Ellie, hunched her slender shoulders. "Sorry, but you weren't paying attention."

"Oh. No, no, I'm sorry, *neña.* You're right." Suave stooped to retrieve the ball from under the table and rolled it across to her side of the net. "I missed, so it's your serve."

"Okay, but you better not be letting me win. I want to beat you fair and square."

Ping-Pong had never been his forte. Evidently, it wasn't Ellie's, either—though the eleven-year-old hung in there, managing to keep the ball in motion. Suave bounced it over her slender shoulder.

"Are you playing Ping-Pong or tennis?" she scolded him.

"Your dad's getting old, baby. Tennis would kill me."

"You're not old, Daddy."

While she hurried after the ball, he looked around for Alina through the crowd of parents and kids.

It was definitely her. Some months had passed since he'd last seen her at Tamara and Diego's wedding. Alina had been assigned to one table at their reception, and he to another. They'd talked maybe for fifteen minutes. As the matron of honor, she wore a sky-blue dress with off-the-shoulder sleeves, which showed off her feminine shoulders. She had worn her dark brown hair up that evening, and he couldn't take his eyes from her smile or the simple gold necklace that drew attention to the kissable skin of her neck.

And why did he remember it that way?

Ellie caught him staring at at Alina as she played a game of skeeball with her son. "You know her, Daddy?"

Smiling, he snapped out of it. "Oh, that's Tamara's big sister. You know Tamara and Diego."

"Yep. Aren't we going to say hi to them?"

"Sure. Sure we will. Why don't we finish our game first?"

"Because we're going to be late for the movie."

"We have time. Wanna play the video games instead?"

"Not really. Unless you want to."

Quietly, he set the paddle down onto the table. There was a time when a high-tech indoor playground like the Funhouse would've entertained Ellie for an entire afternoon. Now his daughter—the child Tracy had conceived with another man, yet given to him—was growing up fast.

She bounced the ball up and down with the paddle, bored. "She's Diego's sister, you said, or Tamara's?"

"Tamara's."

"Uh-huh. And she's like Tamara, too."

"Yeah? In what way?"

"She's pretty hot. *You* think so, anyway."

Suave made a big show of consulting his watch.

"Hey, look at the time. We're gonna miss that movie if we don't hurry." With a hand on her arm, he guided Ellie around the table. "And I don't think she's hot. Well, she is, but she's my friend's sister."

And that was who Alina Romero would always be to him. The pretty, friendly, and elusive girl who crossed paths with him in the school corridors and at Tamara's home. Then, their conversations had been brief, about as long as their chat at the wedding.

"So, why are you looking at her like that?"

"Like what?"

"Like you used to look at Mommy."

This struck a nerve in him. "She's a friend, Ellie. No—a friend's sister. That's all. She's very pretty, but . . . the only one for me was your mom. And now, you're my girl."

Ellie dismissed his hand, which was tenderly ruffling her ponytail. There were traces of her father in her features, but mostly she was Tracy in miniature. The classic, turned-up nose dotted with freckles, the high cheekbones and soft blue eyes—all were from her mother. Even the habit of shaking her head to clear the bangs from her eyes had been mysteriously derived from Tracy.

"I'm going to say hi to her," she said. "It's rude to leave without saying hi, and Tamara will get mad if she hears about it."

"We'll say hi. I never said we'd. . . ."

Alina and Justin moved from the skeeball game to a giant maze of tubes, slides, and mesh pits. Ellie was on her way over to them. Suave didn't know if his daughter was afraid to offend Tamara, whom she'd taken a liking to, or if that little kid part of her couldn't resist the maze.

Kicking off his shoes, Justin got down on his hands and knees to enter the maze through the first tunnel, followed by Alina. Suave walked slower, taken by the sight of her tantalizing rear, clad in tight capri pants, disappearing through the tunnel's opening. Ellie followed moments later.

What he felt was attraction. He didn't have to be a rocket scientist to figure that one out. Alina Romero was seriously pushing all the right buttons in him.

And that would never do. Not Alina Romero, not for a thousand reasons. Firstly, it was downright weird. She was Tamara's sister, and he'd had a bone to pick with the eldest Ms. Romero for quite some time.

All three of them were in the gigantic maze, which took up an entire wall. He knew Ellie liked to hang out in these things, but they had a movie to catch. With resignation, Suave knelt and squeezed his six-foot-three frame into the tunnel.

Alina was his least favorite Romero girl. Tamara had always been number one. Mercedes had been the cute youngest kid he had loved to tease and hoist over his shoulder, threatening to throw her in the pool for being a little pest.

She'd always raised a fuss, screaming for her dad, then punching Suave when he put her back onto her feet.

Alina was the one who deserved to get dunked and taken down several pegs. Out of respect to the parents, he had kept his mouth shut the time that Alina had put down Tracy to his face. Tamara had done the same—but her he forgave, again and again.

Which was none of Alina's damn business.

Tracy es una qualquiera. Forget her, Suave. Every guy in this school, freshman or senior, has gone to bed with her, except for you. And you won't, because even she knows you're too good for her.

In fairness, Tamara had also said similar things about Tracy. *Everyone* talked about the heroine of his heart in those terms. Suave knew Tamara cared for him as a loyal friend, and she spoke out of concern for him.

Alina, on the other hand, was just the high and mighty princess, the pristine and popular good girl, looking down her nose at the bad girl he loved.

"Ellie! Ellie, where are you?"

Somewhere in the distance, through tunnels and slides, a voice cheerfully called back, "Right here, Daddy!"

"Right here. Yeah, right. Where's 'here'?"

He was too big for the maze. Claustrophobia set in, little by little. He was afraid of his shoulders jamming in the tunnel and of getting trapped. Crawling carefully, he emerged through the opening and fell straight into the mesh pit.

"Ellie! Ellie, I don't know where you are, but we have to get to the movie! I hate missing the beginning!"

The mesh was another disaster. There was enough room for most parents—those under six feet—to stand up. Suave couldn't even get a foothold. His sneaker caught on the mesh and tripped him.

"El-lie! Where are you?" Lowering his voice then, he muttered, "Oh, damn, I'm lost in this thing!"

A feminine laugh bubbled over behind him. Not in the mood for levity, he threw a glance over his shoulder.

"I'm not *really* lost. Just lost my bearings for a second."

The woman smiling back at him through the tunnel's opening, with her hair charmingly mussed, was Alina Romero.

"Suave? Is that you?" She beamed, delighted. "Fancy meeting you here. *Que divertido!*"

"Yeah. Very . . . *divertido!*" He tried to mirror the same enthusiasm through his embarrassment. "How've you been, Alina?"

"Fine, fine. And you?"

"Excellent. Never better."

"Good. Hold on. You look like you could use a little help getting out of that thing."

A small cluster of kids, ranging from six to Ellie's age, gathered outside and watched. Suave noticed that they were fully amused by the sight of two adults tangled up in the dreaded mesh pit.

"I'll bet you a dollar the guy doesn't get out," one of the boys told the kid next to him. "And they have to call the fire department to rescue him."

"Na, he's getting out. The lady's helping him."

"A dollar says he can't do it."

"Okay, you're on."

Alina struggled to hold back a laugh, releasing it once Suave reached the opening of the next tunnel and stopped to point at the betting kid's companion.

"Hey, he owes you a dollar," Suave called to them. "Make sure you get it!"

Slipping into the tunnel behind him, Alina bellowed out to be heard above the noise in the tunnel above them. "So tell me, Suave. You come here often?"

"Uh, no. Not too much. And you?"

"Often enough. I'm a little worried. I can't find Justin now."

"He's your son, right? Tamara and Diego tell me he's a sweet little guy."

She smiled. "Most of the time, that's true."

"Well, I can't find my daughter, either."

"Ellie's her name, no?"

"Yep. Ellie." *The daughter of the girl you called* una qualquiera *some years back.*

A term that came dangerously close to *basura blanca*. White trash.

"I hear she's a little doll, too."

"Thanks. Is that the end up there?"

"I can't see. Your—um—*your* end is in the way."

An extremely nice backside, at that, she thought.

Along with long, athletic legs. Alina forced the thoughts from her head.

"Sorry about that. It's some kind of—circular thing, going around and around."

"Oh, that's it, that's it! That's the end."

"Thank God for that, because I have to find Ellie. We're going to a movie."

"And I have to find Justin. He's only four."

The last tunnel emptied into a portal, beyond which spun a drum painted black and white, its swirling colors creating a hypnotic effect. Getting through it would be tricky but not awfully difficult. Suave stood on the portal beside Alina; crowding her in an area meant for smaller bodies.

"Think you can handle that?" she asked.

"That's kid stuff."

"I'm dizzy just looking at it."

He conceded. "My turn to help you."

Suave grasped her forearm, leading her into the final part of the maze. Then things went downhill after the first step, with both of them losing their footing. Alina fell first. Suave struggled against the laws of physics and lost, falling on top of her.

It was a tangle of arms and legs, and they ended up in a compromising position, with one on top of the other. Alina yelped and laughed, grabbing Suave's shoulders and saving his glasses before they slipped from his face. Her hand brushed against his cheek, and she felt the heat of his skin on her fingertips.

She saw black and white and the color red from

somewhere—a fiery, vibrant red—and the brilliant blue of his eyes, much too close to hers. His mouth was moist, ripe for a kiss. *One kiss, from a man's mouth.* As he fought to help balance her, she leaned closer to him, reveling in the sinfully wonderful taste of his kiss.

Two

A current of heat lingered on Suave's lips after their mouths parted. The huge drum they were stuck in continued its dizzying rotation. He was sufficiently light-headed, needless to say, without any help from Alina Romero's wayward mouth.

"Damn, girl. What'd you do that for?"

Her big eyes got even bigger, and she shook her head. Her long hair was wildly tousled, sex-kitten style. It was too much for him to endure.

"No—no sé, no sé lo que. . . ."

As one of his father's pet sayings went, *"el diablo se le metio en el cuerpo."* The devil must have invaded his body, too, because the next thing Suave knew, he was cupping one hand around her face and lowering his mouth onto hers. The devil— sure, that was an acceptable excuse. The devil made him lust after another too-sexy-to-pass-up kiss.

Later, he'd probably regret surrendering to the impulse. For now, he waited for Alina to regain her common sense and release her- self from his kiss. Instead, her tongue hungrily sought his, in a wild, surprising show of blatant desire.

What am I doing? Alina heard the question in a part of her mind that was still miraculously functioning. Kissing was a thing of the past. Sisterly pecks on the cheek for friends or Tamara and Mercedes were one thing. Her son, father, and two brothers-in-law composed the list of men entitled to her kisses—those of the chaste variety.

Chaste was not the right word here. And she was kissing Suave Rivera. Tamara's old friend—more of a nuisance than anything else when she came home from school and found him hanging out with Tamara in the kitchen, pretending to study over pound cake and Doritos. Not that anything of a romantic nature had ever happened between them. In essence, Tamara cherished him as the brother she never had, given to her by friendship.

Awkward, hopelessly nerdy Suave. Nursing a case of unrequited and undying love for that girl—what was her name again?—the school's resident bad girl. He had been saved from true geek status by his talent out on the basketball court.

Who was this sexy hunk expertly slam-dunking her emotions, and what had he done with the real Suave?

A voice that hadn't yet reached puberty brought them back to reality. "Told you they'd start that kissy-kissy stuff." Half-dizzy, she looked out of the cylinder to see the betting boy snatch a dollar from his friend's hand. "Gimme that back."

The faces of their uninvited audience spiraled before her eyes. One belonged to Justin, who was staring at her curiously. Another belonged to a Funhouse attendant, stony-faced and severe, arms folded beneath an abundant bosom.

"There are kids behind you trying to get out of the maze," she ordered. "Would you two please move it? Now?"

"We were trying. . . ." Alina jerked out of Suave's hands, inching toward the opening. "But it's not as easy as it looks."

"Even harder when you're tangled up in some-one's arms." The matronly woman helped Alina to her feet, letting Suave fend for himself. Look-ing her in the eye, the woman said, "Just for your information, this place is rated G. Next time, can you and your husband please wait 'til you get home?"

"He's not—we were just leaving, in fact. My son and I are leaving." All Alina wanted was to get out of there—and the sooner, the better. Off balance from the kiss and the motion of the drum, she al-most reeled backward into a little girl waiting her turn to enter the maze.

She steadied herself and took Justin's hand. "Let's get our shoes, *papito,* and let's go."

"Alina, wait up—don't go."

Completely light-headed, Suave lost his bal-ance. Ellie glared at him and unfolded her arms in an effort to catch her dizzy dad, toppling over with him onto the floor.

"You two okay?" Alina touched the girl's arm. "Here, honey, let me. . . ."

Ellie yanked her arm away. "I can get up by my-self!"

"Alina, Alina, wait a second. Did you, uh, like—"

"Yes, it was fun—it was *nice*, I mean, seeing you again, Suave. I'll talk to you soon."

She hoped and prayed that would only take place with her younger sister and brother-in-law around to act as chaperones. Rushing, she trailed a confused Justin by the hand behind her to the cubbyholes where the shoes were stored.

"I don't want to go," her son argued. "Wanna stay here for a little while longer."

Alina frantically searched for Justin's Sesame Street sneakers and her black espadrilles. Some of the other parents had witnessed her and Suave's indiscretion in the maze. Most had just shaken their heads, but one one spunky grandfather appeared fervently amused.

"We have to go, Justin. I have to pick up stuff for dinner."

"But Abuelo's making dinner. He's making *arroz con pollo.*"

"That's right. And he makes it so delicious, we don't want to miss it, do we?" Gently, she placed the sneakers onto his little feet. "I'm sorry, *papi*. We'll stay longer, the next time we come. I promise."

Justin wasn't pleased. He slouched into a orange plastic chair and set his little chin stubbornly.

"Tomorrow, can we come back?"

"Not tomorrow. I have some things to take care of. But maybe Abuela will take you to the playground in the afternoon."

What a terrible thing she'd done. And there was no way she'd have time to finish tying Justin's second sneaker and get her own shoes on before Suave came up to her. His long legs moved pretty fast. Ellie dragged her feet behind him.

According to Tamara, Suave had lost his wife a handful of years earlier. Whatever had happened in that maze was simply inexcusable—and disrespectful. She hadn't really considered him or his daughter . . . or her son.

Yet, he had felt so good in her arms. His body against hers, even fully clothed, was warm and strong and compellingly masculine. His sensuality was impossible to resist, but it was still wrong and uncharacteristic of her.

He towered imposingly over the back of Justin's chair, regarding her darkly.

"Alina, I asked you to wait a minute," he said, sternly. "And you just ran away from me."

"It's okay, really. It's no big deal. We'll talk later." In a hurry, she thrust her left foot into her right shoe, kicked it off, and scrambled for the other espadrille. "It shouldn't have happened."

"No, it shouldn't have."

"I don't know why I did that."

"I'm as much to blame as you are."

Irritated, she nodded at Justin. "Suave, can we please talk about this later?"

"Better yet, let's not talk about it at all. Let's forget it happened."

She winced at his cool tone. "Okay. Yes, better idea. I'll never bring it up in conversation, if you don't."

"I won't, *nena*. Believe me."

His stare was on fire. Subsequently, Alina's equally fiery Cuban-Dominican temper blazed up.

No me digas! She didn't bother to inform him that he'd been far from angry when his tongue was in her mouth back in the maze.

"You know what? We've said . . . all there is to say, I think," she spat back at him.

"I think you're right."

"I think so, too."

"You said that already."

Waving her hand in the air in frustration, she huffed, *"Está bien, ya.* I'll see you. Or maybe I won't."

A look of hurt crossed his face, but then he quickly composed himself. "Either way would be fine with me, Alina."

"Sounds good here, too, then. Let's go, Justin."

Suave pushed his glasses farther back on his nose, watching Alina helping Justin back under the turnstile at the indoor playground's exit. Ellie stood to his left, her hands on her hips, pursing her lips sullenly.

Great. Another temperamental female for him to contend with!

"And what's your problem, *jovencita?*" he demanded.

Never in her eleven years had her adoptive father ever raised a hand to her. He didn't have to. Her mother had occasionally swatted her on the behind, but Suave had never spanked Ellie. Misbehaving usually called for some time-out in her room and the loss of TV and playtime privileges.

It rarely came to that, however. All Suave needed to do was employ a strict, deep voice, and Ellie heeded it. She did so now, albeit reluctantly.

"Nothing. We're going to be late for the movie." She stalked off to track down her sneakers, biting back preteen fury.

"I've never been to this place, the Funhouse. But it sounds like a fun place to take Tamara." Diego Santamaria chuckled at his thinly disguised insinuation, shaking salt liberally over his french fries. On the other side of the booth, Suave picked disinterestedly at his *caldo gallego*.

"It's a kiddie place, bro," he explained.

"Sure doesn't sound like it."

"No, come on—video games, skeeball, air hockey, you can grab a pizza and ice cream—"

"And don't forget the 'Maze of Love.' I'll tell you, they didn't have places like that when I was a kid. Not in Chile, anyway." Diego swallowed a mouthful of his *medianoche* sandwich, waving one hand theatrically in the air. He was on a roll. "That's very poetic, you know, Suavecito? 'The Maze of Love.' Love is a maze. How profound."

"That wasn't love. I can't explain what happened in there. One minute, we were fine, trying to get out of that thing and find the kids. The next minute"—he dropped his spoon beside the soup bowl, giving up on it—"we were getting tossed around on that ride, all over each other. Naturally, I held on to her and she held on to me—"

"Naturally."

"—and then she kissed me. Instead of stopping her—you think I would've done that—I kissed her back. Hard. It was like I was an animal, like one kiss wasn't enough. I had to have another one."

Diego growled. "So it became the 'Maze of Lust.' I want the address of this place, before you go back to work."

"Well, I'm glad you find this so funny, but I'm missing the joke. Tamara's big sister came onto me. That's what it amounts to. And I thought maybe you could shed some light onto what happened for me, since you know Alina better."

"I don't know how I'd do that. You've known her longer than I have. But I don't want you to walk away disappointed, so I'll try to be a good advisor." Good-naturedly, Diego polished off his sandwich, dusted his hands with the cloth napkin, and sat back in his chair. "First, you need to tell me something. If a beautiful woman makes an advance, why shouldn't you respond in kind?"

"Again, we're talking about Tamara's *sister.*"

"Yeah, I'd agree with you if it had been her mother. Then I'd say, 'Suave, you have a problem.' But so what if it's her sister? Don't you find Alina attractive?"

"That's the whole thing. I don't."

"Oh, no? If you didn't find her attractive, why did you kiss her back?"

Impatiently, Suave glanced through the window at the Horizon Beach Savings Bank clock across the street. Fifteen minutes of his lunch hour remained. He was going back to work at the shop without an inkling of what to do next. This had been a waste of his time—and Diego's, who'd taken a break from writing his latest novel to meet him at the restaurant close to the office.

He then decided that the best thing was to be entirely honest with the man. They'd become close friends as a result of Suave's childhood friendship with his wife.

"All right. She's attractive. But it doesn't matter."

"Why's that?"

"Because I don't like Alina." There. The truth was out. No taking it back now.

Stunned, Diego leaned forward. "You don't like her? Why not?"

The truth, the whole truth, and nothing but the truth, he chided himself, hoping he could truly trust Diego Santamaria. "Oh, it goes way back. She's very conceited, for one thing. She thinks she's 'all that', as Ellie would say. She always did."

"Alina? Really? I think she's a sweetheart!"

Suave was immediately on the defensive. "I know her better than you do. You said that yourself. You didn't know her in high school. It's a loyalty thing."

"You're being loyal to somebody by making Alina the enemy? Who're you being loyal to, exactly?"

"Uh . . . Tamara, for one."

"Tamarita?" Diego shook his head. "Suave, Tamarita loves her sisters. Alina, just as much as Mercy. Those three are real tight."

"Well, now they are, yeah. But there was a time when Tamara felt ... I don't know ... overshadowed by Alina. And Alina's the spoiled daddy's girl, out of the three of them."

"At one time, that was true, granted. Now Alina's grown up, and so is Tamara, so I don't think my wife really expects you to keep defending her to her sister." The humor returned to Diego's eyes. "In other words, if you want to roll around in the 'Maze of Lust' with Alina, it would be with Tamarita's blessing."

The waiter dropped by their table to collect the dishes. Diego ordered some espressos. He sat forward in his chair, rubbing his hands together.

"This isn't really about Tamara, though, is it? You have something else against Alina. What would that be?"

"Before I answer that, is any of this going to get back to your wife? I don't want her to have a bad opinion of me."

Diego gestured emphatically. "Whatever you say stays between you and me. Man to man."

At ease, Suave nodded slowly. He'd sincerely liked Diego from the day he'd first met him, before he married Tamara. An avid reader, he'd admired the best-selling Chilean-American author's work, long before learning Diego was romantically involved with one of the Romero girls.

"You're probably going to tell me it's stupid to obsess about things that happened a long time ago. But one day, when we were teenagers, we were sitting together in the kitchen, and Tammy was there with Alina and her mother. And to make a long story short, Alina had some things to say about the girl I was in love with that weren't very nice."

Diego listened quietly. The waiter passed by again, placing a demitasse cup in front of each of them.

"This is the same girl I ended up marrying. Ellie's mother. Alina called her *una qualquiera*. And maybe she was, to other people, but Tracy was never that to me. And you're probably amazed that I'd let that bother me for so long."

"No, I'm more amazed that my mother-in-law didn't tell her oldest daughter to behave herself and mind her own business. Carmela's usually spunkier than that."

Appeased, Suave smiled. "Maybe it's foolish, but every time I see Alina, I remember those words."

"*Claro que sí*. Someone could have said something to us, or done something, years and years ago, and we still see the shadow of it right behind them. That's human nature. We save the hurt, even if it eats us inside." Understanding, Diego sipped his espresso.

"And the strangest part was, when I saw her at your wedding, and when she kissed me in the maze, I wanted her."

"This goes as far back as our wedding?"

Suave nodded begrudgingly. "It goes back further than that, but I don't have time to get into it. I have to go back to work."

"Oh . . . yeah," Diego checked his watch. "You do. Finish your coffee. And I'll tell you what you should do."

"Please do. The suspense is killing me."

"I'm supposed to meet Alina this Friday at a house she's thinking of buying. Her and the real estate agent showing the property. Just to, you know, check the place out with her."

"And?"

"And you're gonna take my place and meet her there, instead." Seeing Suave open his mouth to argue, Diego stopped him. "Ask the guy questions about the house, then get her by herself. And then you're going to tell her off. Be gentle but firm. Tell her exactly how you feel, just like you told me right now, and get it the hell off your chest."

"That's not such a good idea."

"Why not? I think that know-it-all teenager, that spoiled daddy's girl who was so insensitive to you, has been through enough pain in her own life now, enough to realize that she hurt you. It wouldn't be fair of you not to give her a chance to make amends and to just go on, holding a grudge indefinitely."

"I can't do that."

"I'm afraid you have to. You owe it to Tamarita. And buddy, you're gonna pay up in full in that area, because she loves you *and* her sister, and she'd be so unhappy, knowing there was something wrong between you."

Suave insisted on picking up the check, walking out onto the avenue minutes later with Diego. The rain had stopped shortly before they'd entered the restaurant, and the sun was trying its best to reappear. They strolled the three blocks to the office leisurely, swinging their umbrellas at their sides.

"Okay. I'll go in your place on Friday," he agreed. "I'll talk to her about it then. Not that it'll do any good."

Laughing, Diego patted his back. "Why are you so sure of that? Give her a little credit. She's not a teenager anymore."

"No, that she's not."

"And neither are you."

"Ah. Speak for yourself!"

And what a teenager Alina Romero had been. One of those unattainable girls, unless a guy's status was worthy of her. Even being a stellar player on the basketball team hadn't helped him, when that proud and well-known girl dismissed him as Tamara's good-hearted best friend, about as exciting and interesting a flavor as vanilla.

After saying good-bye to Diego, Suave entered the office building through the loading dock and proceeded down the hall to the A.J. Preston Printshop. His skills on the presses had landed him a job there upon his return to the East Coast. In a matter of months, the day supervisor had his eye on him, already talking about Suave as a candidate for foreman.

He sighed, opening his locker and taking his navy-blue smock off the hook. His experience and knowledge as a pressman, earned from years at another shop in Nevada, as well as being a member of the union, had won him a better-than-average salary. It wasn't an exciting job, nor was it his lifelong dream, but it paid the rent on the modest apartment he shared with his daughter and kept them well fed. That was what he got, he supposed, for foregoing college to join the very pregnant woman he'd loved.

He regretted nothing. Suave would've hopped that plane again in a heartbeat. The one advantage to his job was that he enjoyed working with his hands—the satisfaction of actually having something to show for hours toiled—yet there were other things he would've preferred to be doing. Some days, he feared that he'd grow old before ever getting a chance to attempt them.

Were he actually to pursue a relationship with Alina, what future would there be in it? One Romero sister had married a wealthy, best-selling author and lived with him in a gorgeous, huge house; the other, a multimillionaire who chose to work with troubled kids as a counselor and played clubs with his rock-and-roll band rather than run his father's corporation. Suave liked them both— Diego Santamaria and Quinn Scarborough, Mercedes' husband. They were down-to-earth, regular guys.

Yet they were still on different level, financially. What did he have to offer Alina? Her husband hadn't been a famous author or a rich kid with a guitar. Marco had earned his living as a firefighter. *Watching her sisters live the good life had to have some sort of effect on her,* wouldn't it? he mused.

He went to his press, preparing to mix the ink before running the job that would take the rest of the afternoon to complete.

It wouldn't be fair of you not to give her a chance to

make amends and to just go on, holding a grudge. . . .
He remembered Diego's words with a pang.

Suave had seen something besides a shadow.
Something shining through her eyes. Passion.

He wasn't prepared to see that in Alina Romero—not directed at him.

Three

Alina walked slowly from her car to the short stone path leading to the house. Whether it was Tamara or her brother-in-law, one of them was going to hear from her later.

Mr. Peterson had called in sick. His replacement was a petite, African-American woman named Shauna Hodges, who wore a chic business suit. During their phone conversation, the woman had been very friendly and amicable, and she didn't mind being joined by another family member at the home. She had arrived at the address before Alina, and her white BMW was parked in the gravel driveway.

The impression that Alina got of Shauna from their brief dealings was that she was no Mr. Peterson. She wasn't going to undermine a potential buyer simply because she was female, which made it unnecessary for Alina to have her brother-in-law there at all.

Except that Diego was nowhere in sight. It seemed Mr. Peterson wasn't the only one with a substitute. Standing beside the the house, examining the exterior and windows with his head tilted back, was Suave Rivera. The very last person in the world she wanted to see.

Exactly what did Tamara and Diego think they were doing? Or maybe it was an honest mistake. She came close to confiding in her sister about that scene at the Funhouse, then decided against it. Her lack of trust wasn't toward her sister but rather herself. Alina was afraid to hear the words coming from her mouth, almost as fearful as she was of the excitement flowing through her upon seeing Suave again.

She had kissed him and he kissed her back—and she'd loved it. He had invoked pleasure, raw and uninhibited, in her at that moment. However wrong it had been, she'd been thrilled at having a man like him in her arms, the two of them overwhelmed with tenderness and surprise. Such a long time had passed since she'd felt that way. Alina felt almost powerless against it, and that alone scared her.

She slowed down, trying to remember the younger Brendan Rivera. The one who had been no match for her, an unsure boy a few years younger than her, his face marred with acne. He had been the shortest kid in his class, then sprouted up at around the age of fourteen until it seemed he'd never stop growing.

As a kid, he hadn't cared much about his appearance, donning any old T-shirt and jeans and ragged sneakers, his hair constantly in need of a good trim. His glasses were no help, either.

Time had sculpted a man out of a boy. From the side, his profile was nothing short of heart-stopping. He was good-looking in a rugged sort of way, and his complexion was clear. His build was naturally lean, but his chest, arms, and shoulders had filled out, tapering down to a trim waist.

Funny how the glasses didn't detract from his looks any more. At the maze that day, she'd noticed how well he fit into his jeans, and how perfectly his nickname suited him.

Suave. More smooth than soft, easy on the eyes and in an embrace. Like music that put a woman in the mood, or the mesmerizing lull of the ocean's rhythm, or a glass of brandy that warmed the body, its power to intoxicate going unnoticed before it was too late.

That sort of man—what was he like in bed? And why did that question preoccupy her, first on that afternoon in the maze and now, when he was here?

She had no immediate answer, and was grateful for the distraction when the real estate agent rose from one of the front steps and approached her.

"Mrs. Oceguera?" She offered her hand. "Shauna Hodges. Very nice to meet you."

"The same here." Alina smiled. Out of the corner of her eye, she saw Suave approaching.

"May I call you Alina? That's such a lovely name."

"Of course."

"Good! I'm sure you're aware, but it seems your brother-in-law wasn't able to make it this evening, so he asked Brendan to come instead." Shauna searched her face for approval. "Will that be all right?"

Suave leaned over Alina's shoulder. "Yes, will that be all right?"

She whipped her head around, nearly smacking him in the face with her long hair. "That's great . . . Brendan. I appreciate that."

Armed with the house keys, the agent sprang into sales mode.

"What do you say we go in and check this baby out?" she chirped. "I know that Arnold, my esteemed colleague, gave you the first tour, but sometimes love can strike at second sight rather than first. . . ."

A step behind her, Alina twirled around and whispered to Suave, "What happened to Diego?"

"I'm sorry, Alina. I missed that. What'd you say?" Shauna asked.

Alina turned to face her. "I said, that probably is possible, love at second sight."

"Let's hope so. For the house's sake, that is," Suave muttered. He inspected the foyer and living room. "Good size. It's bigger than it looks like from the outside."

The agent threw out her arms. "You know, that's what everybody says, when they walk through that door. Nice and big, lots of living space!"

"Hmmm. Why so dark, though? And what are the walls like, behind that wood paneling?"

"Dark? Um, yes, but the windows are a great size. Lots of . . . of potential for"—Shauna tried unsuccessfully to open one of the windows, which rattled noisily—"For light to come in. And those walls are good, old-fashioned plaster underneath."

"Uh-huh." Suave said nothing, making his way to the mantel. "And this is a working fireplace?"

He was taking his role as amateur home inspector seriously. No doubt about that. Admirably, he kept the agent on her toes.

"It hasn't been used for a while, but yes, it does work." She appealed to Alina. "Nice feature, isn't it? You like sitting in front of a hearth on a cold night? That's what you call built-in romance."

That particular agent couldn't have known. Alina had been dealing exclusively with Peterson, who either was really out sick or he'd considered giving her a second tour as a waste of his time. Perhaps he hadn't told Shauna his client was widowed.

Yet Suave knew. He glanced at the woman, then rested his eyes on Alina. His silent inquiry said, *Are you handling this all right?*

Alina smiled at him.

"Very romantic, yes. I've been living in Florida for a few years, so I miss those cold winter nights."

"Oh, Florida? You lived down there? I went to the University of Tampa."

Shauna chatted as she led the way through the first-floor rooms. Alina chose to drift into the background, allowing Suave to ask questions and put Shauna on the spot, with the same polite yet firm attitude that Tamara had employed.

As she heard about how old the plumbing was and whether the electricity was up to modern code, love for the house failed to bloom at second sight. On the other hand, a different spark of interest was born in her.

The dining room whispered what memorable dinners a table would bring to it. The kitchen hadn't always been so dark and gloomy and outdated. The elderly couple who were selling the house had been young once, and a family, years earlier, had bustled between that room's walls before leaving for school and work.

Suave was doing about as well as the house at charming her. Rather than behaving as if the task were imposed upon him, he seemed genuinely enthusiastic about helping her come to a decision.

Whatever lunacy had assailed them both at the indoor playground reappeared when they reached the upstairs and entered the master bedroom. Suave was getting the first view of the room her bed would be in, where she'd sleep alone, if she were to buy the house.

"You can get a king-sized bed in here comfortably," Shauna was saying. "And, oh—I love this! A window seat! Really, they just don't make houses like this any more. And you can see the whole backyard from here."

Alina lifted her eyes to see Suave's gaze fixed on her. It was the same look as in the maze, a split second before he had devoured her mouth in an impetuous, fabulous kiss. The memory proved too much for her, and she shook her head self-consciously.

"So, uh . . . what do you think?" she asked him.

"It's not what *I* think. It's what *you* think. You like the house?"

"I do, but is it . . . is it worth the money?"

"It'll be money just to fix it up, but it looks like mostly cosmetic stuff to me." Grinning, he motioned to Shauna. "Let me know if Alina doesn't buy it. I'm in the market for a house, too, and this would do fine."

Pleased, Shauna laughed. "Alina, you'd be wise to decide. I can honestly tell you I have another buyer who's interested."

"I can see that. And he's trying to take my house right out from under me." Alina rubbed her neck. It was time to take the plunge. "When can I place a bid?"

The agent put on a poker face, aptly disguising her zeal. "You can meet me back at the office now. I'll work up the contract and present it to the sellers tonight."

"Then I guess I'm buying this house"—she jutted her chin at Suave in playful retaliation—"before somebody else makes you a better offer."

"That's wonderful! You won't regret it. This place is a wonderful old lady."

Over a hundred thousand dollars for a house. Alina took a deep breath as Shauna locked up and breezed away to her own car.

You just bought yourself and Justin a house. By yourself. Almost by yourself.

Suave stayed with her in the front yard, remarking on the property's strengths and weaknesses. She watched him carefully for any sign of attraction. On the contrary, he was living up to his name; he was smooth as smooth could be, sounding nonchalant and sticking to the subject at hand.

It was driving her crazy. What was going on with her? This hadn't happened with any other man—not since Marco.

Suave was a problem.

Waiting for a break in the conversation, she said, "Well, I don't want to keep the agent waiting for me at the realty office."

"Yeah, I know. You'd better get going."

"I appreciate your taking the time to join me here, Suave. You were very helpful."

"Sure. Don't mention it."

He went off in one direction, and she in the other, fishing for her car keys in her purse.

"Alina!"

Her stomach flip-flopped, and she held on to the car door for support as he walked toward her. He'd called her name forcefully, like a command.

Or a proposition. He was so unlike that younger, shy, gawky Suave Rivera. But people had the tendency to change over the years—and not always for the best.

"Forget something, Suave?"

"No. That's just it. It's something I'm having trouble forgetting."

Alina fidgeted with her purse strap. This was going to make any future encounters doubly uncomfortable.

"To be totally honest with you, Suave, I don't know what happened that day. It . . . it didn't mean anything, so I hope you don't think that . . . uh, anything's going to come of it."

His gaze grew stormy. Fixing his hands onto his waist, he vented an exasperated sigh.

"You know, Alina, I'm really trying here, but— aren't you the presumptuous one? *Still?*"

She tossed her purse into the car. "I'm trying here, too, okay? But what I'm saying is that if you came here, expecting—well, I don't know what you were expecting."

"Oh, I agree. I shouldn't have expected anything at all from you. And I'm not gonna say anything else, out of respect for your sister." He slapped his arms to his sides. "But what'd you think? That I came here because I was so bowled over by one little kiss from the great Alina Romero?"

"I assume we're talking about my heyday, which is over. Being in with the popular crowd in high school doesn't mean much in the real world."

"I know. But you miss that, don't you?"

She paused. "Yes and no. Yes, I miss believing I was as special as everybody made me out to be, back then. And no, because it wasn't true. I was just like everybody else."

"Well, maybe not like *everybody* else. You were a bit more privileged than some."

Alina leaned against the car, squinting at him curiously. *"De quien hablamos?"*

"De Tracy."

"Tracy? Tracy? Your wife, Tracy?"

"The one and only."

"I don't understand what she has to do with this."

She was being sincere. She had no clue, no recollection, at least for the moment. What Suave wanted was to drop the whole subject, head to his own car, and get out of there. He ventured closer to her, resting his back against the car.

"Alina, I didn't come here because I thought you were some hot-to-trot widow, for God's sake," he told her, softly. "As I recalled, I kissed you back, so I'm just as guilty. But that's not what this is about. I came here at Diego's suggestion, because I told him—"

"You told him what?" The panic showed through her voice. "You told my brother-in-law about what happened at the Funhouse?"

"I told him a little more than that."

"Oh, no, Suave!"

"Alina, listen up. Forget that. There's something more important I have to tell you." For emphasis, he jabbed a forefinger into the air. *"Es algo que pasó ya, hace años, pero te lo guardo. Te lo guardo."*

He held something against her? She was quiet, permitting him to go on.

"I guess it boils down to that it's important for me to tell you that . . . Tracy—who *you* once told me was a *qualquiera* and who you didn't have a very high opinion of—was a good wife to me, Alina. A good wife, and a loving mother to our daughter. I bet you wouldn't have thought she'd turn out like that, being the way she was when she was younger, but she did."

"Una qualquiera . . . I called her. . . ." She stopped, her voice now a near-whisper. "I did. You're right. But, Suave, that was years ago—"

"I know, I know."

"Come on. Tamara said the same thing—"

He raised his voice slightly. "And your sister was looking out for me. It was different when she said it, I don't know why. Besides, Tamara didn't have your power in school. I know you got together with your perfect friends, the beautiful people, and you whispered about Tracy any time she passed you in the hallway. She heard you guys. And what you said about me . . ."

"I said you were too good for her!" she defended herself, then held her tongue.

Suave narrowed his eyes at her. "You also told Tamara that I didn't have a chance with Tracy. That Tracy didn't want a decent guy, that all she wanted was someone cool and good-looking to bed her. And that hurt, Alina, on both counts."

Speechless, she shifted her weight to the other foot. "How did she die?"

"She had congenital heart disease. When she was twenty-five, she had a massive heart attack. They tried to perform surgery to repair some of the damage, but Tracy died on the table."

"Oh, God. Oh."

"Anyway, I just wanted you to know that. I don't expect an apology, Alina. I don't have a right to one—it's been years. But I wanted you to know,"—his voice cracked mildly—"That I knew she did wrong when she was younger. I wasn't stupid. But Tracy had it tougher than you did, growing up, and she didn't have much self-esteem. But she was as good a wife and mother as I'm sure you became."

"Oh. Oh, Suave. I am so, so sorry."

He took a deep breath. "I said you don't have to apologize."

"Yes, I do. It was . . . stupid teenage-girl stuff, but," she said, touching his arm, "I'm glad she straightened out. And I'm sure you had a hand in that, too. But for the record, I do apologize for what I said about her. I never knew how much it hurt you."

He was astonished. Alina, apologizing to him? Humbling herself only added to her dignity, a trait that had always been so evident in her.

It also confused him. The old Alina he knew, or so he thought. Then again, the old Alina wouldn't have wanted to kiss him, either, then draw another one from him of his own volition.

This new Alina was so much more complicated, and she had so many more facets to her character. It made her all the more real to him—too real for comfort.

"Well, I accept your apology."

"Do you?"

He cracked a smile. "Yeah."

"Good. But now you owe me one."

"Why's that?"

"Because you forgave Tamara, but not me. Now I feel hurt!"

The statement won a chuckle from him. He'd refrained from physical contact with her, just in case, remembering what had happened previously only too well.

But his upbringing betrayed him. Both his parents were loving, his Puerto Rican father in particular. The elder Rivera believed that, sometimes, the only response was an embrace. Sometimes words left much to be desired or they became garbled, but a hug translated perfectly, every time. A touch of the hand or open arms said, "I love you," or "Don't worry, everything will be fine" as well as it could express, "All is forgiven."

Between a man and a woman, there was always the danger of misinterpretation when it came to that sort of physical expression. Yet, Suave threw caution to the wind, offering her his open arms. Hesitantly, Alina accepted.

A fast and quick hug—she knew that was the safest way to go. Lasting no more than a couple of seconds at the most. But when his arms encircled her waist and hers found comfort around his neck, she wondered if she could ever let go. It was more than the arousal caused by her breasts pressed against his chest, protected only by the fabric of his shirt and her blouse. That alone was disarming—the signals that her body was sending her, agitated pleasantly by everything, his touch, the scent of his cologne, the ardent protection of his arms.

It was something else, a connection between his soul and hers. She closed her eyes tightly, hoping to will it away. It was probably one-sided, anyway. A hug was a hug. Certainly, to a man, that was all it could be.

She felt his body relaxing against hers, the curves and contours of her body fitting his splendidly. She was afraid of that. Afraid, too, that he might feel her heart's acceleration, placing her in such a vulnerable position.

Wisely, Suave broke the embrace.

"You better go and, uh"—he cleared his throat—"get that bid in on your house."

"Uh-huh, that's right. Okay. Thanks again, Suavecito."

"Hey, my pleasure."

He began walking away, and she opened the car door, sighing.

"One more thing, Alina."

"Yes, Suave?" She leaned out of the car to acknowledge him.

"About what happened in the Funhouse. . . ."

"Yes?"

"I haven't had a kiss that beautiful in a long time."

"No, Suave. Neither have I."

She closed the door and started the engine. It did nothing to drown out the schoolgirl cheer of glee hiding deep in her chest.

Four

Regardless of the fact that Alejandro Romero had his own key to the basement apartment, he preferred to respect his daughter's privacy and knock at the door. Alina set the soup ladle down and hurried to let him in.

"You got back pretty quickly," she said. "Boy, you move fast for *un viejito!*"

His laugh was deep and rich with age. Handing her a bag from the pharmacy, he said in a heavy Cuban accent, "That is your mother's doing. All those vitamins that she makes me take. Vitamins for the bones, for the blood. She and I, we are never going to die, with all those vitamins."

"Eh, Mami's a smart lady. And you're smart, for listening to her." She removed the bottle of Children's Tylenol from the bag. "Let me pay you back for this, Papi—"

"No, *digo, tranquila.* Anything for my grandson. How is he?"

"I got the fever down a little bit, but not much. This should do the trick, though. If not, I'm calling the doctor again. Justin's inside."

"I'll go see him. *Mi bandolero!*"

"Okay, and I'll be there in a minute."

Once in the kitchen, Alina loosened the bottle's childproof top and plucked a spoon from the utensil drawer. She lowered the flame under a pot of soup simmering on the stove. She was fixing chicken-and-stars soup, Justin's favorite. Maybe that would help his appetite, since nothing else had been able to in two days.

Her parents' nicknames for Justin helped to raise her spirits. To her dad, he was *el bandolero Justin*. Her mother called him *mi rey*. Watching his boundless energy sapped by what the pediatrician diagnosed as a case of gastritis, Alina just wanted to call him "healthy" again.

She walked in on grandfather and grandchild visiting together. Alejandro sat on the bed, wiping Justin's hair away from his forehead.

"I'm not hungry, Abuelo," her son told him.

"Not hungry? No? *Papito*, you will feel better if you eat. It's soup."

"Not hungry."

"Not thirsty, either," Alina observed, checking the glass of lukewarm ginger ale on the nightstand. "Drink a little bit more, honey."

"It tastes yucky." He crinkled his small nose at the spoonful of medicine headed his way. "No, that's yucky, too."

"No, it's grape. You like grape."

Justin shook his head, snuggling closer to his grandfather for protection from his medicine-wielding mother. Alina chuckled.

"I know, I'm sorry, but you have to take it, okay? It'll get the fever down."

Alejandro imparted a piece of advice. "You close your eyes and you drink it fast. Don't let it stay in your mouth."

With Justin's cooperation, she spooned the purple liquid into his mouth. He looked ready to spit it up, but he bravely tossed his head back and drank it.

Justin's color worried her. She'd never seen his face so pasty, even through colic and bad colds and middle ear infections—all the childhood diseases she'd lived through with him. He was a good eater, to his grandparents' delight, yet he wouldn't take even a nibble of anything. This was one of the most stubborn fevers she'd ever tackled.

"I'm gonna sleep. Okay, Abuelo?"

Another cause for alarm. Justin, napping so much? Napping ceased for him at the age of two. A tad hyperactive, he was a little man of action, not to be held down by naps when there was a whole, exciting world out there to explore. With the gastritis—or whatever it was—he slept on and off during the day.

Alejandro joined her in the kitchen. She reached for a plastic container from the cupboard to store the soup in as soon as it cooled.

"*Café*, Papi?"

"*No, gracias, mi amor.*" Wearily, he sat at the table. "If he is still like that later—"

"I'm going to run him over to the emergency room," she finished his statement. "The pediatrician closed the office early today."

"I'll take you there. And you, Alina? How are you?"

She poured water into a teapot and set it on the burner. "Eh, Papi, when he's sick, I'm sick."

"Hmmm. He'll be okay. You're the one who's going to end up in the hospital."

"Yeah, you always say that," she teased, bringing out a mug and a teabag.

"No, it's true. Mercedes told me she thinks you should go to the house by the lake."

"And, don't tell me, let me guess. You think Mercedes is right?"

Alejandro was entertained watching her prepare a cup of tea. One tea drinker, in a whole clan of coffee lovers. Alina picked up the preference in college from a roommate who didn't touch any form of coffee bean. He scratched his head of silver hair, addressing her question.

"A weekend. Not even the whole weekend. Friday and Saturday. You'd come back Sunday. *El bandolero* stays with me and his Abuela."

"Mercedes wants me to leave him with her and your son-in-law." Wiggling her fingers at him, she sat down. "I'll let you two work that out."

"You're going, then?" He was pleased. "I'm glad. Before you start in the new school, with everything in your life right now. . . ."

"Oh, I know. A lot in my life, Papi. You have no idea." She studied her nails.

"What you mean?"

The Romeros loved all of their daughters equally. Yet there was a special bond between Tamara and their mother; Mercedes was their loveable youngest; Alejandro was both father and friend to his firstborn. She confided in him easily, in whatever circumstance she faced.

"Papi, there's been something happening to me lately," she began. "I don't know how you're going to feel about this. But there's a man that I feel . . . I feel something with him. I'm not sure what."

"Oh, yes?" His smile was radiant. "Who is this man?"

Alina groaned, breaking into a laugh. "You don't want to know."

"What does that mean? It can't be anyone bad. I know you, Alina," he responded confidently. "You're too smart for that. Now, you have me curious. So who is it?"

"Brendan Rivera."

"Brendan Rivera? Who is that?" Then recognition beamed in. "Oh, *Suavecito!* Him?"

"Yes, him. Isn't that strange?" She posed the question more to herself than to him.

"Pretty strange, yes. I always thought he would marry Tamara, not you."

"Well, hold on, Papi. Nobody's getting married here." Alina laughed. "As a matter of fact, I should really ignore those feelings because that's the wise thing to do."

Her father adamantly disagreed. "Why do you think that's wise? Alina, you're not going to be alone forever, are you?"

"That's the whole point, Papi. Sometimes, I feel alone because Marco's not there anymore. Maybe that's what's happening here. And Suave is in the same boat, because you know that his wife died, too."

"Listen to me. At your age and Suave's age, you don't grieve forever. You don't have to be lonely—"

Alina interrupted. "No, but you should be with someone because you love them, not because you don't want to be alone. It's not fair to the man, and it's not fair to the woman."

"Oh, Alina, for once, you're wrong." Folding his hands loosely on the table, her father went on. "That sounds very serious. I'm not talking about love. I'm talking about getting to know someone better. Sharing good times with them. Discovering that you have something in common with them. Finding that you have the same values. Feeling happy with that person. You know what I mean?"

On the table next to the napkin holder, the cordless phone rang. Alejandro reached for it first.

"You give yourself that much permission, and maybe later, you give yourself permission to love again," he concluded, speaking next into the phone. *"Digame.* Oh, hello. Yes, she's here."

"Who is it?"

"Shauna from Alliance Realtors."

Shauna hadn't been able to reach the sellers for days. They had been visiting their son in Georgia for a week and had neglected to inform the realty office. Another day was lost while Shauna handled two other closings. Something had happened to Alina in the interim, during which she passed the house each day, seeing it only from the outside. The more she saw it, the less its faults seemed to show, and the more it resembled a good, friendly home for her little family.

It was a set-up for disappointment. Whether she was ready for it or not, this was her answer. She held the phone to her ear with a breath caught in her throat.

"I'm calling you on my cell phone," Shauna said after the preliminary small talk. "And I just left the seller's."

Alina tittered. "Shauna, you're killing me with the suspense."

"I know, Alina, and you've waited long enough to hear. They were very happy with your offer. You've got yourself a house. Congratulations!"

"Oh—I don't believe it!" She laughed with the agent, turning to her father. "The deal went through on the house, Papi."

Her father rose from the table in response to the tea kettle's whistle. *Vaya! Felicidades, mija!*

Shauna was rattling off instructions faster than Alina could process them. The main things that stood out concerned obtaining an attorney, the mortgage going through, and smooth sailing ahead from there.

She hung up the phone as her father finished making her tea and set the mug in front of her.

"We have to make a big dinner to celebrate your new house," Alejandro announced.

"You mean my *old* house. Wait 'til you see it."

"It's old?"

"Old . . . and beautiful." Rising, she added, "I'll be right back, Papi. I'm going to go check on Justin again."

"I'm going back upstairs. I'll give you and my grandson time to celebrate alone."

Mortgage. What a frightening word, she reflected, entering the bedroom she shared with Justin. In Florida, housing cost less than here, and her teacher's salary and Marco's firefighter pay had been enough. Now, the monthly payments would depend on one person: her.

What had she committed herself to?

Shauna had told her that Alina had an attorney review period, and she was able to recommend a very good lawyer. *A lawyer. More money.* The math kept getting more complicated, what with the home inspector, the application fee, and all of the other out-of-pocket costs. Checks written out, cash depleted slowly but surely from her savings account.

Then, once they'd moved into the place, what if the roof sprang a leak and the hot-water heater died, and the kids next door shot a baseball through one of the first-floor windows? Would she have the money for the repairs?

She'd considered all the financial ins and outs of buying a house before she'd ever contacted a realtor, resulting in the decision that she *could* do it—barely. Maybe it wouldn't be easy—more of a sacrifice in many ways—but it was possible.

It wasn't the first time worries about money had assailed her since Marco's death.

Alina had hated the nights following her husband's funeral, when she'd taken hours to fall asleep, wondering how she'd make ends meet. She also despised occasionally buying a lottery ticket in quiet desperation, praying not for the big jackpot but for just enough money to act as a buffer.

It wasn't enough that she had to get used to life without Marco, which was more heartbreaking than anything she'd known. No, she also had the future—hers and Justin's—weighing heavily on her shoulders.

The only good to come of it was a lesson in independence. How carefree she'd been as a kid, depending on her parents; later, she'd shared the responsibilities with Marco, the other half of her team. Maturity came with a price—the loss of innocent dependence—yet she was coming to understand that independence was daily practice in trusting in herself.

She could harbor self-confidence in her instincts as they directed her to a major decision such as buying a house. Why, then, couldn't she trust her desire for Suave Rivera?

Justin was asleep, and she sat on the bed. A hand to his forehead indicated that he was burning up, though he'd drawn the bedcovers up to his neck and was shivering in his slumber. His labored breathing sent dread seeping through her, and she returned to the kitchen for the phone.

"Papi, can you come back down here, please? No, everything's okay, just—it's just that I need you to drive Justin and me over to the emergency room . . . as soon as you can."

One by one, Suave ruled out each lame excuse designed to prevent him from dropping by the hospital.

He stepped out of the elevator onto the hospital's third floor, following the signs marked PEDI-ATRICS. The most convenient excuse was time. His immediate reaction when Tamara mentioned over the phone that Justin had been admitted to the hospital was that there'd be no chance for him to get there.

No chance? With the hospital within walking distance of his job and his lunch hour available?

One of the four nurses at the nurse station asked him a question with upraised eyebrows. As he passed, Suave answered by holding up the cardboard visitor's pass and continuing down the corridor to Justin's designated room.

First of all, not finding fifteen minutes to drop by seemed so cold, certainly not his style. Secondly, he knew what it was like having a child in the hospital from when Ellie had her tonsils taken out. He understood what Alina was going through, between the worrying and the challenge of entertaining a bored little kid stuck in the hospital.

Another reason he made the time to be there was from a sense of compulsion. Suave couldn't figure it out, but he felt compelled to show his face to see for himself that Justin was fine now and to offer support to Alina.

He walked through the doorway of room 321 to find mother and son in bed with pillows propped up behind them. They were leafing through a large, ancient photo album together. His footsteps interrupted them.

Alina looked up, her smile instant. "Suave! What're you doing here at this time of day?"

"Visiting my friends. Actually, I'm dropping somebody off."

He stood to Justin's left and freed a small toy dog from the gift shop bag in his hands. The boy's face, having regained its healthy color, brightened. Suave crouched slightly, holding the stuffed animal in one hand and bobbing his head up and down.

"Yo, man, wazzup?" he said, adopting an urban inflection in a squeaky voice. "I hear you sick!"

Fascinated, the boy shifted closer, careful with the IV needle in his arm.

"I was sick. Now I'm better," he replied to the toy but smiled past it at Suave.

"Yeah, yeah, I can see that! I was down in the hospital store. Isn't this place mega boring?"

"Yeah. I hate it."

"Aw, me, too. When you're ready to go, can you take me with you, man? I'm gonna, like, escape."

Alina laughed and closed the scrapbook.

"When I leave, I'll put you like this," Justin demonstrated by tucking the toy under his Poké-mon pajama top. "So they won't see you."

"Hey, I knew you were the man to come to!" Grinning, Suave kissed the boy's forehead and spoke normally. "So your *Tia* Tamara told me you were dehydrated, huh? Didn't drink or eat enough?"

"No. And I should've pushed him harder to do both of those things," Alina offered.

Recognizing the strain of guilt in her voice, Suave disagreed gently with a shake of his head.

"We parents do the best we can," he insisted. "He looks good now."

"Now, yes, and the IV's coming out later. They're releasing him tomorrow."

"Well, good for both of you." He pulled up one of the two armchairs in the room. "Now that's one of those *old* babies," he said, referring to the photo album.

Alina said, "No kidding. Made in Cuba, probably around the 1940s. Papi's family. Justin's never seen it, and God help me if I don't bring it home intact—"

"You're running out of things to do in here. Been there, done that." He held out his hands. "Can I see it?"

Alina obliged. "Don't mind the pages. Some of them are loose, and a few of those corner things they used to paste the pictures in back then are lost. But it's an heirloom, believe it or not."

"Oh, I believe it." He pushed the cover open gingerly, noticing the frayed, burgundy-velvet fabric. "Any news on the house?"

"The agent called the same night they admitted Justin. I got it."

"All right! *Felicidades, nena!*" He nodded at Justin. "Congratulations to both of you."

The boy set the stuffed animal on his lap, saying proudly, "I get my own room."

"That rocks. You deserve your own room, little man." Suave gave him a thumbs-up. "That's gonna be a great house to grow up in, too. Are you happy?" This was addressed to Alina.

"It hasn't sunk in yet." She laughed. "And then

with Justin being sick . . . I'm happy, but I'm scared."

"Tell me about it. If I ever find a house for me and Ellie, it'll be the first home I own. I've lived in and out of apartments all my life." He focused on the photo album to tear his attention away from Alina's face. "Who says the world isn't black and white? It was back then."

"I like those black pages, too. Very dramatic. I find the pictures kinda sad, though." She sounded subdued. "They say, 'This was my father's Cuba, when she was free.' "

Suave was silent. He didn't have to speak. Alina read his expression as compassionate, and that look filled her with a comforting warmth. Just seeing Suave again soothed her.

"That's my *abuelo*," Justin said, jabbing a pudgy finger toward a snapshot.

"Which one is he? Show me again, buddy." Suave brought the book closer to the child. "That's him, huh? Boy, your abuelo was a good-lookin' devil!"

The boy smirked, whispering, "And skinny, too!"

Alina listened to the hearty roar of Suave's laughter.

"We won't tell him you said that. But, hey—looks like he's still got that same head of hair. We'll give your grandpa that much."

"And he makes good banana milkshakes."

"Yeah, and you know why? You know that story, Justin?" He waited until the boy responded with a shake of his head. "Your grandpa used to sell them on the street in Cuba. He earned a little money for his family that way back then."

"Really?"

"Yep. That, and I think your aunt told me he made underwear, too."

Scooting off the bed, she rearranged the balloons, cards, and Matchbox cars sent or brought by her family on the windowsill. She didn't want to let on how captivated she was, witnessing the interaction between Suave and her son.

Naturally shy, Justin had taken time to warm up to both of his uncles. He was more of a ladies' man in his boyish way, thinking nothing of hopping onto a woman's lap and fiddling with any available necklace. With men—perhaps because they were usually larger and gruffer—Justin seemed to feel them out more before getting too close.

Was this the result of his father dying when he was barely out of diapers? Alina hoped not. His grandfather was an exception—Justin's choice for best buddy—and Diego and Quinn were now within his inner circle. For Suave, however, the child had broken his own rules.

Was it because he was also a father? Or was it Suave's nonthreatening approach? Children sometimes instinctively know when adults simply tolerate them and when they sincerely like them.

Suave was soft-spoken and easy-going. He had a funny side to him, evidenced by his ability to make a stuffed animal speak, as well as talking to Justin on his own level.

It was the first time she'd seen that side of Suave. To her chagrin, Alina found it completely irresistible.

"And your father sold milkshakes in Cuba?" Justin asked him.

"Mine? No. My dad lived in Puerto Rico. That's Cuba's neighbor in the Caribbean. He had a cool job, too, though."

"What?"

"He used to take care of the horses that belonged to this really, really rich man in San Juan. He used to let my dad ride them all the time. Fun job, right?"

"You ride horses, too?"

"Me? No." He laughed again. "I rode a horse once, and he tried to jump the fence with me on him. That was enough for me. But . . . I do build some cool miniature towns. I'll show them to you sometime, if you'd like."

Justin was intrigued. "When?"

"Whenever. Let's wait 'til you're out of here first, bro." Closing the photo album, he set it on the nightstand. "I have to get back to work, so the next time I see you, you'll be all better with that needle out of your little arm."

"I don't like this thing."

"I wouldn't, either. They do some weird stuff to you in the hospital, eh?"

Alina straightened the band on her wristwatch. "I'll walk you down to the elevator. I want to get a cup of coffee, anyway. Justin, *papito*, Mami will be right back."

I can do this, she coaxed herself. Something as

simple as walking alone with him down the corridor to the elevators without succumbing to the excitement of seeing him again. It was the easiest thing in the world. She'd ride down the elevator with him, thank him for coming, and they'd part in the lobby.

"A miniature town?" she asked, after pressing the down button.

"My second, actually."

"Uh-huh. Interesting hobby."

"First time around, I made Las Vegas. The hotels and everything. My boss liked it so much, he bought it from me."

They heard the *ting* of the elevator bell before the doors opened, and they stepped in.

"And what town are you working on now?"

"A no-name town. Just a little hometown. My idea of a nice place to raise a family." Suave grinned and pressed the button for the main floor. "Like I told your little guy, you can come see it whenever you want."

He held his hands at his sides, dug into his pockets, and then withdrew them. The elevator moved like molasses, lengthening his dilemma. Alina was quiet; she wasn't exactly jumping at his invitation.

It was just as well. He didn't want her thinking he had ulterior motives in coming that afternoon or that she was in any way obligated.

And then he remembered.

"Except for next weekend, Alina. I'm going up to your parents' summer house, the one by the lake."

"Oh. You are?"

The button marked M lit up in red, and the elevator eased to a stop.

"Well, yeah. Tamara's been offering me the key for a while, and I finally took her up on it. She's watching Ellie for me, too."

Alina's head was spinning as she walked off the elevator.

"It's—it's very peaceful up there," she remarked.

"Exactly what I need. Peace and quiet for a couple of days. I haven't had time to myself in—well, I can't even remember how long."

And you're going there alone? That question was off-limits.

What if he were taking a woman up there? In all the times she'd seen him, he had yet to mention if he was seeing anyone. A pang sliced through her, and it felt a lot like jealousy.

He ended her reverie by stopping in his tracks right in front of her.

"You don't mind, do you, Alina?" He kept his voice low and cool.

"Mind what?"

"That Tamara loaned me the key."

"Oh, no, of course not. I've been thinking about . . . a weekend like that, too. You know, leave Justin with Mercedes and Quinn, get my head on straight. When he's well."

Suave nodded. "If you'd rather have it next weekend, I could wait. It belongs to you. I'm just . . . peacefully trespassing."

"It's not mine. It's my parents'. So if I showed

up there too, we'd both be trespassing. Peacefully."

"I'd have no objections to that. At all."

Alina's jaw dropped open slightly. She was teasing; he wasn't. She also had her answer, without embarrassing herself to pose the question.

There wasn't a woman in his life—other than that little woman, his daughter.

She said, "I don't know if that would be as peaceful as it would be romantic."

Suave studied her for a long moment. "I could make it both for you."

He kept his hands to himself and a distance between them. Regardless, the heat and electricity flowing between them shot a thrill through her.

"That sounds an awful lot like going away for the weekend. *Together,*" she clarified.

"Nothing like that. I'm going to be there, for sure. If you decide to go, we'll be there together. I'll leave it up to you. But, Alina, I keep thinking that you. . . ."

She blinked. "That I what?"

"Nothing. I gotta go. Take care of Justin."

"Okay. And you take care of Ellie."

It was difficult for her to breathe as she boarded the elevator again. What was he going to say to her? What was it that he kept thinking about her?

In effect, he'd asked her to go away with him for the weekend. Alone, in a lakefront house, hidden away in a secluded, wooded area. A home that had only one bed in one bedroom, where more could be happening than throwing fresh fish on the grill.

And she'd said no. She'd pulled away out of fear. The only man she'd ever been intimate with was Marco. He had been the sole object of her desire.

How strange and frightening it was to feel desire again. And for this man, who'd never been a stranger to her.

Five

The greatest injustice in life was that, of all four seasons, summer was the shortest.

Come September, those halcyon days would end with school opening its doors to students and faculty alike. Then it would be back to the classroom, brown-bagging lunch, and working on grading test papers and assignments in the evenings.

For now, Alina relaxed in the salon, listening to the club music playing over a speaker while the manicurist worked on her hands. Tamara sat at the next table getting French tips.

It was so ironic how the years had reversed the two women's roles. Before, Alina had been the high-maintenance one, keeping regular appointments to have her nails and hair done and so up-to-date with the latest fashions.

Her sister had been the sporty one in high school. Tamara always looked good, whether on the girls' basketball court or at a dance. Yet she was interested in other things that didn't include trips to trendy shops or a hairstylist who saw her every six weeks.

Now it was Tamara who was starting her own magazine and becoming the fashion plate in the family. Alina didn't feel jealous but rather a passing melancholy.

Wasn't that the way things were, though? She was getting older. Fourth-graders needed a teacher, not a model—although the boys wouldn't have minded if the teacher looked like Tyra Banks. She bought her clothes off the rack based on whether they were practical, comfortable, and mix-and-match. Finding time to squeeze into her busy schedule for a French manicure at this stage in her life seemed out of place.

This is what had sent her out with Tamara. An hour at the manicurist, another hour at lunch—and then she'd taken Justin to the boardwalk for a while before dinner.

Tamara examined her free hand. "You don't even have to call Mercedes, you know. Mami will give you her key."

"Oh, God. I knew I shouldn't have said anything to you," Alina groaned.

"I'm not saying anything. I'm just making a suggestion, if you do want to go up there. Why go all that way to get it from Mercy, when Papi has a spare set. Unless. . . ." Smirking, Tamara said, "You don't want him to know you're using his house as a little love nest for you and a *man*. Jeez, he would've thought me or Mercedes capable of that—not his angel, Alina!"

Alina wasn't in the mood for teasing. "Forget I said anything, Tammy."

"Oh, okay. I will."

"I only told you because I thought, as his best friend, you would know what he didn't want to tell me."

"I was best friends with Suave, the teenager. I've been getting acquainted with Suave, the man. They're the same, and yet they're different."

Me lo dices? To give the matter as little importance as possible, Alina looked away. "Has Suave, the man, said anything to you about it?"

"Not to me."

Her older sister went a different route. "Maybe to your hubby?"

"If he did, Diego didn't mention it to me."

"And if Suave did confide in him, and Diego told you, would you mention it to *me?*"

Tamara tilted her head. "Are you asking me if I'd betray my close friend's confidence by reporting everything he said to my sister?"

"No. That's not what I'm—"

"In a New York minute. For you, there's very little I wouldn't do, Alina. But I can't give what I don't have—and I don't have any info from Suave."

Those statements touched Alina. She avoided the subject throughout the rest of the manicure, waiting a few minutes in the shop for Tamara's nails to dry.

There was a time when Tamara would have sided with a friend from school instead of her big sister. Her relationship with Mercedes had never been strained. There had never been a time when the baby of the family considered herself in

Alina's shadow—the main thing that aggravated the situation with Tamara.

Yet, as their mother was fond of saying, her daughters were three apples that fell from the same tree and proceeded to roll as far as they could from each other. Alina reflected on this philosophy as she walked with Tamara down Main Street toward the boardwalk.

They were each other's flesh and blood, close and fiercely devoted sisters. Yet at the same time, they were utter individuals, or "originals," as Papi put it. Mercedes, the young dreamer, was the most generous with her affection between the two. Alina normally would have found her youngest sister's arm linking through hers as they walked.

The dreamer, Mercedes, and daddy's girl, Alina, were easy friends from the start. But daddy's girl and Tamara, daddy's rebel, had gotten into their share of teenaged catfights. And two *latinitas* at war, armed with matching, fiery tempers, could go at each other something wicked! Aside from the clash of personalities, Alina took an all-knowing older sister role, and Tamara defied her at every turn. Papi didn't help things, either, occasionally using Alina's top-notch school grades and decision to settle down after college with her new husband and child as examples for Tamara to follow.

As an adult, Alina understood her sister's position better than her own when she was younger. Tamara didn't want to be traditional; she wanted to soar on her own wings, and she didn't want anyone telling her to pattern her life after anyone else's.

The sibling rivalry eventually diminished. The sisters really talked to each other now about personal hardships and triumphs and everything else under the sun.

There wasn't one particular incident or time that caused the healing of their relationship. No dramatic climax, no overly sentimental Hallmark moment. Just two sisters, over the course of time, discovering a loyal friend with open arms in each other.

Tamara broke through the small talk once they set foot onto the boardwalk. "He used to have a little crush on you, you know."

Alina widened her eyes. "Who? Suave?"

"No, that chubby guy over there, *el gordito*, sunning his sexy bod on the beach!" She giggled. "Yes, Suave! This is before he ever laid eyes on Tracy."

"What did he say back then?"

"What the world always said about you. That you were so beautiful and you looked like one of those Spanish flamenco dolls people had in their houses—remember them?"

"Sure. How could I forget? Those and the ugly, red ceramic bulls." Alina laughed.

"Yeah, like the one we had in the living room. God, I hated that thing! I cheered when Mami made Papi throw it out!"

"Okay, it was ugly, but Papi swore it brought us good luck." She stopped to pinch Tamara's arm. "Now, get back to what you were saying . . . about Suave."

Tamara eyed her deviously. "You know who you reminded me of right now? Those friends you had in school who wanted to know every last detail if you found out something about a guy they liked."

"Don't be silly. I'm just curious."

"Are you? Too bad. Because you never ran to me to talk about Marco. You ran to your 'mature' friends—but I love it that you're coming to me now."

Who said that Mercedes had to corner the market on affection? Alina took the initiative, hooking her arm through her sister's and drawing her closer as they strolled. The water was calm that day, lapping playfully at the wet, darkened sand. A young boy, around eleven or twelve years old, gave up on catching a perfect wave and glumly toted a boogie board back to his family's beach blanket.

"This is so crazy," she said, more to herself than Tamara.

"He once asked me if you would say yes if he asked you out."

Alina didn't hesitate. "When was that?"

"When we were real young. You were already a star in school, and we were peons."

"And what did you say?"

"I said, 'I doubt it. She only goes out with the popular crew.' "

"You were probably right, too. Then he forgot all about me when Tracy came along."

"And he loved her, and loved her, and loved her. As much as you loved Marco. But now Tracy and Marco aren't here any more, and enough time has passed for both of you that you're seeing each other with new eyes." Tired of walking,

Tamara drew Alina to a bench facing the beach. "So I ask you, what is so crazy about that?"

Off in the distance, a beach patrol dune buggy rolled across the sand. Feigning interest in it, Alina hesitated.

"He wouldn't have told me to be there this weekend," she said, "if the feelings weren't mutual."

"Of course not."

"But it's just that—I can't do this. I really don't know how. How do you go away with someone for the weekend? How do you do that? I've never done that. I went away with my husband. Period. He was my husband by the time I went to bed with him."

Tamara shrugged. "Well, you don't have to have sex. Make that point as soon as you get there."

"So what's the point in going, then?" She blurted it out too quickly, unable to stop herself, collapsing into spontaneous laughter with her sister. "No, but it's true. I want him. I want to get to know him better, like I've never known him before—but I also want him, physically, as a man. That's what really scares me."

"What's to be scared of? You open your suitcase, pack a nice perfume—oh, something very alluring and tempting, that you can dab here, and here, and don't forget, *here* . . ." Wickedly, Tamara pointed at her ears, her neck, and the top of her cleavage. "And you throw in something wildly sexy, preferably black or red. Black, if you're feeling romantic. Red, if you're feeling especially naughty."

"Lingerie." Alina pursed her lips.

"Uh-huh. Revealing, but leaving something to the imagination."

"I haven't bought lingerie in a long time, Tammy. No use for it."

Softly, Tamara said, "That's all right. Lingerie only has one purpose. To tell a man, in a pretty hot whisper, what he already knows—that you're a woman. It usually whispers to you first when you get it on your body."

Quiet for a moment, Alina then smiled. "Well, from my experience, I know it has one more purpose."

"Getting yanked off and tossed on the floor in the heat of passion. You pay a pretty penny for something you wear for two seconds before he says, 'Oh, baby, you're delicious!' and slides it off you. And *that's* Victoria's *real* secret!"

Alina looked away from a casual game of volleyball on the beach to her sister's face, sighing. "I don't know if I can do this. But I want to be touched again. And I want it to be Suave's hands that touch me."

"You don't think this is scary for him, too?" Tamara moved closer to Alina, her tone poignantly gentle. "He's the one who laid his heart out on the table by asking you to join him up there. I'm sure that, after Tracy and before you, he hasn't made a single move like that."

"I'm gonna call you tonight and tomorrow, okay? See how you're doing."

Suave kept one eye on the road and the other on his daughter seated in the passenger seat beside him. Ellie nibbled on a plum she'd grabbed from the kitchen table before leaving for the ride.

"If you want to," she said. "It's only the weekend, Papi. You worry too much."

He flicked on the turn signal, easing the car into the right lane for the exit. Even with eleven years of experience as a father, kids were still hard to read.

"That's because we're hardly ever separated," he told her.

"But I'm staying with Tamara. You know I'm going to be okay. And I've slept over at my friends' houses before."

Yeah, and you can thank your mom for that, he wanted to say, smiling.

When Ellie was seven, Tracy had won that argument. Suave didn't realize how many of his father's ways had integrated themselves into his own parenting style until the topic of sleepovers became a debate. His old-fashioned dad wasn't keen on a child sleeping at someone else's home other than family.

When she was eight, Ellie had pleaded to sleep over at a classmate's home. The elder Rivera, over the phone, had agreed with his son—but Suave's modern American mother got on the line and told him, in no uncertain terms, to stop being so archaic.

In the end, it was Tracy who put her foot down, saying yes to the sleepover. As Ellie's adoptive father, Suave had grumbled but backed down and spent the night wondering if a fire or something would break out in the classmate's home.

"You're not mad at me, right?"

Ellie rolled her eyes. "For what?"

"For going off and leaving you for a couple of days?"

"Papi, we're not attached at the hip, you know." She dropped her annoyance and smiled at his laughter.

"I know that, *mama.*" Swinging his arm behind her headrest, he added, "But you'll understand when you have kids of your own."

"Yep, that's what you say all the time, whenever you forget I'm not a little kid any more."

"Maybe because you're in such a hurry to grow up and be independent." *And it scares the hell outta me.*

"I'm gonna have fun at Tamara's. I'm never coming out of her pool, and you're going fishing. That is what you're going to do there, *riiiight?*"

Was that accusation in her tone? He glanced at her. "Excuse me?"

"Nothing."

"No, don't you give me that 'nothing' jazz. What do you think I'm going up there to do?"

Wrapping the plum pit in a napkin, she shrugged. "I don't know. Meet a lady, maybe?"

Suave was about to deny the charge but stopped himself. Lying to his little girl simply wasn't in him.

Instead, he was cautious. Never give out more information than a kid asks for. "What makes you think that's gonna happen up there?"

"Because this is the most excited I've ever seen you get about fish. And nervous."

"I'm not nervous."

"Yes, you are. We had to go back to the house twice. First, because you forgot your fishing license. Then, because you forgot the *rod!*" Ellie turned to him, sternly. "Makes me think fishing's not the real reason you're going."

"That could happen to anybody." He was immediately sorry after blurting the words out. "What if I did meet someone there, Ellie? How would that make you feel?"

Diego and Tamara's house came into view and she stared out the window. "I don't know."

"No, you *do* know. Talk to me, baby."

Ellie sat ramrod straight, watching him pull the car into the driveway. She adopted her "cool kid" stance and shrugged again.

"Why do you have to have a girlfriend?" she asked.

"I don't have a girlfriend. Yet. Now you answer me this"—he cut the engine, nodding at her—"Why are you going to have a boyfriend someday?"

"That's different."

"Is it? You gonna love me less when you love your husband? No, right? Your love for me and your love for him will be different. Doesn't mean you'll love either of us less."

"You have a girlfriend!" The expression on her reddening face was a mixture of disappointment and anger. "It's Tamara's sister. That lady you kissed in the maze and went to see in the hospital. You're meeting her at the lake."

"She's not my girlfriend. And as far as I know, I'm going up to that lake by myself."

Diego appeared at the end of the driveway, backyard hose in hand. Ellie waved through the windshield, returning his friendly smile with a less hearty one.

"Just a minute, baby," Suave said, stopping her hand on the door handle. "I want to say one more thing."

"What, Papi?"

He shifted toward her. "I was there when you were born. And I'm always gonna be there for you. It doesn't matter who comes into your life or mine. You're my little girl, and nothing and nobody can ever change that."

Clutching her small hand in his larger one, Suave saw her face soften.

"But if I ever brought anyone else into our lives," he continued, slowly, "it would only be a very special lady. Somebody who I knew was gonna treat both of us right, and love you and me very much. We're a package deal, baby. You want one of us, you get us both."

Ellie pushed her hair, falling loosely in strands from her scrunchie, behind her ears. Suave felt a tug at his heart as he watched her bite her lower lip, giving herself time to choose her words.

"I still feel like. . . ."

Diego walked toward them and peeked in through the open passenger window. His hair was in disarray from an industrious day spent in his spacious backyard. He greeted them with gusto.

"Hello, beautiful houseguest!" Eliciting a smile

from Ellie, he scowled at Suave. "And who's that ugly guy next to you?"

"Don't listen to him, baby. He's just the gardener!" Suave teased.

"Hi, Diego!" Ellie sang out.

Opening the car door for her with a flourish, Diego held out his hand and gallantly helped her out.

"Hey, I got the pool ready for you," Diego said. "And your *Tia* Tamarita's coming right back. She went to pick up some Malta Goyas and hamburger meat to make *pastelitos de carne* for us."

"Yummy! But I never had Malta Goya. What's that?"

"A soda. You never had Malta?" Bending over, Diego looked into the car. "*Oye, pero, cabellero*—and you call yourself a Latino dad? Shame on you!"

"Hey, she's had Cola Champagne and she loves it. Okay by you?" Chuckling, Suave stepped out of the car.

"I got my swimsuit under this," Ellie told Diego, sticking a thumb under the strap of her shirt. "Can I go in the pool now?"

"Sure! As long as I or *Tia* Tamara is back here, you can go in the pool whenever you want. That's your only rule for the pool, sweetie. Somebody's gotta be back there with you."

"Okay, Diego!" Ellie agreed, skipping down the driveway.

"Hey, wait up!" her father called. "*Un beso, no?*"

Running back to him, she hugged his waist. Suave bent his frame over her, embracing her more tightly than usual, and received an endearingly sloppy kiss on the cheek.

"Have a nice time, Papi."

"You, too, El. I love you."

"I love you, too." She threw in one more kiss, then ran off to the spectacular swimming pool that was hers for the weekend.

Diego slapped him lightly on the back. "You staying for lunch, or. . . ."

"Thanks, but I've gotta get going. I have about a two-hour ride from here." Suave sniffed. "You really don't mind, having a little houseguest for a few days, turning into a prune in your pool, finagling you into changing the radio station so she can listen to Britney Spears—"

"We don't mind at all. You go, relax, have a good time."

It hurt him, getting back into the car and driving away. It hurt to leave Ellie, even when he was satisfied that she'd be in good hands.

Initially, the idea of time to himself at the upstate New York house sounded wonderful. It was healthy for him and for Ellie, who'd loved Tamara and Diego's huge, beautiful home from the first moment she'd seen it.

Was it possible to have a good time alone? And if Alina showed up, would it evolve magically into the best time he'd had in a long time—with another adult, specifically?

A sign on the road's shoulder told him he was a mile from the next highway stop. He decided to stop, get a Coke, and then drive straight through to the Romero lake hideaway.

Alina wasn't going to come. He could feel it in his bones that she wouldn't arrive, either before or after him. The realization was a letdown after days of looking forward to seeing her again.

He really needed to get her out of his mind. Why had he gone out on limb and invited her to join him? Now, every time they found themselves in the same room, it would feel weird between them.

What would have to happen for her to be there? An alignment of the planets? Neptune in the house of Scorpio?

Or something as basic and human as her desire to be with him to be as great as his desire to be with her?

No. Not again. He wasn't doing that a second time in his life. He wasn't falling in love with a woman who wasn't in love with him. That had happened the first time around with Tracy, and God knew, he was so young then. To be young and hopelessly in love was one thing. It was quite another to be a man who expected and wouldn't accept less than a woman who was equally in love with him.

But . . . what if she showed up? If she threw caution to the wind, said yes to something so spontaneous and crazy as a romantic weekend—what would that mean? That she was capable of falling in love with him? And what would happen?

Oh, what could *happen!* A sweet and erotic sensation stirred in his body. That was the thing about Alina; he could envision himself in the same bed with her, making love to her, losing his mind touching her. Alina's body, her hands, her breasts, her mouth, all over him. Him bringing her pleasure and her pleasing him.

With a prospect like that, who needed fishing?

What troubled him was that there had been women after Tracy, women he hadn't slept with but who'd tried to lure him into their beds. Two women in Vegas and one in Jersey, since he'd been back, who learned he was a young, available widower. He'd felt nothing for them, no stirring of the body or soul, so he'd walked away for fear of leading any of them on.

Yet for Alina, he felt something. A big something with the potential of being dangerous enough to become love.

I want you to get married again someday, Suavecito. Tracy's announcement had haunted him as he searched for a parking spot close to the highway stop's entrance. That talk took place on the drive home from the doctor's office, days before her death.

If something happens to me and I don't come home, don't you dare mourn for me forever, you hear? Don't you dare grow old by yourself. Fall in love with somebody who deserves you, Suave. Somebody in love with you.

His legs felt heavy beneath him as he walked through the entrance doors of the store. He pulled a handful of change from the pocket of his shorts.

And take care of our daughter. Not "my" daughter, but "our" daughter. He'd never loved that woman more than when he'd heard those words from her mouth.

It seemed impossible once, but now there was another woman working her way into his heart, whether she knew it or not.

And it felt good, so good, to feel that longing again. But realistically, she wasn't coming. The most he could look forward to was the fragrance of pine in the air, the earth beneath his feet, and a nice, fat trout at the end of his line.

Six

It was two o'clock in the afternoon, and Suave still hadn't arrived.

Alina busied herself unpacking her suitcase, using half of the bedroom dresser for her things. Her modesty was challenged by the act of placing her panties into one of the smaller side drawers.

That made it official. She'd gone to the cabin to spend the weekend with Suave Rivera ... who was going to see her undies—and more, if the weekend was a success.

It had been a long time since she'd been to the cabin. It possessed a delightful familiarity that comforted her, with all the traces of the loved ones who'd spent previous weekends there.

That was Mercedes' jar of moisturizer left on the bathroom vanity. The razor blades in the medicine cabinet were Papi's. Mami's Tito Puentes CD, with the original recording of "Oye Como Va," was still in the CD player. Notes scribbled on a sheet of paper, presumably pertaining to a fictional character, had been penned by her literary brother-in-law, Diego, and left behind on the cof-

fee table. The fax in a corner of the living room
belonged to Tamara, who might have sent something to her new business partner and former employee.

Shortly before Alina had left with Mami's key,
Tamara had handed her a huge box, neatly
wrapped in colorful paper. Taped to it was a
sheet of paper that advised: OPEN IN CASE OF EMER-
GENCY!

Tamara, the eternal troublemaker! Alina laughed,
gingerly stowing the gift on the top shelf of the
bedroom closet. She kicked off her sandals,
brushed her hair into a loose, single braid, and
headed into the kitchen.

"Careful with those cabinets," her brother-in-
law, Quinn, had warned her. "I found a little crit-
ter in there, eating a box of Cheerios."

Quinn had failed to mention what type of "crit-
ter" lurked in the cabin's kitchen, and Alina
wasn't very anxious to find out. A field mouse or a
mole, probably; this was the great outdoors, after
all. Mustering her courage, she checked the cabinets and was grateful to find that someone had
cleaned them out before leaving. She began storing bottled water and some Bacardi coolers in the
refrigerator.

The cabin was in good shape, except for a thin
layer of dust on the floor. Alina swept the floor
with a broom from the pantry, tidying each room.
The cabin's central air, which she'd switched on
upon entering, had circulated quickly. As she
swept, she heard a car approaching the property.

If Suave was close enough for Alina to hear him

coming, then he was close enough to see her car parked in the driveway. Alina froze with the broom in her hands, alerted to the moment of truth.

She'd hoped that he would have arrived first, which would have given her something of an advantage—as if she'd left late and had decided to go at the very last minute. As it was, she could still say she forgot their conversation, thought the place was his the following week—or any of a thousand ludicrous lies.

What are you? Eighteen years old and playing games? she thought.

His car stopped outside as she returned the broom to the pantry. Determined, she walked to the door, loosening her hair from its braid. What were pretenses for, anyway? What was the point in them, whether at age eighteen, twenty-five, or sixty-five?

There was an attraction between them, which hadn't been there before. He'd invited her to join him at the cabin, and she made the trip to be there as a mature and consenting adult woman. End of story.

Suave stood with his arm draped over the open door, looking at her car. Alina let the screen door slam lightly behind her to get his attention as she walked outside.

"Have trouble finding this place?" she called out pleasantly.

He let his eyes settle on her and smiled.

"No, I—I got a late start," he replied. "Diego's directions were pretty precise."

"They usually are. He's good at that."

Nodding, Suave gave himself time to think of something else to say. He was still coming to grips with the idea that he'd invited a lady for a weekend-long date—he'd never really done that before—and she'd complied. A lady who stood with the sunlight in her dark hair, highlighting the sheen of its natural flecks of red. Her khaki shorts were sexy over trim, eye-catching legs. Her olive complexion brought out the light hue of her hazel eyes, and the womanly features of her face surpassed the femininity and allure of the teenage beauty he remembered.

There was only one thing to say.

"You know, you *still* look like one of those gorgeous, Spanish flamenco dolls some Cubans have."

Momentarily stunned, Alina tossed him a saucy grin. "Well, thank you. So long as I don't look like one of those ceramic bulls they keep right next to the dolls!"

"Aw, no, no. You don't look like that." Removing his travel bag from the trunk, he walked to the porch steps. "I'm glad you decided to come, Alina."

The thought was like a torpedo, going straight from her head to the pit of her belly. *If anything happens in the next couple of days, it'll be with that body.* He was close to hers now, wearing cut-off denim shorts and a short-sleeve, navy blue T-shirt. He had a good body—one of those truly *machito* bodies, towering and imposing and muscular. Suave was so tall, he made her head instantly dip back on her neck, which added to her vulnerability.

"I brought some . . . some stuff with me." She avoided acknowledging his thanks. "Nothing much. Just some cookies and *bistek de palomilla* to throw on the grill."

"Hey, sounds good! So did I. I stopped at a store before getting off the highway. Not much— we'll be having some fish from the lake, I hope."

Did their greeting merit a kiss? Suave had absolutely no idea. Her pretty face was tilted up at him, perhaps in anticipation, but she wasn't initiating anything.

That left him, as the man, to do the honors. Bending slightly at the waist, he aimed for her lips but landed on her nose, embarrassing himself with a loud, smacking kiss.

Alina clutched the porch railing and her eyes danced with amusement. She was giggling inside. That was like a kiss from an awkward high-school freshman.

Man, am I ever out of practice! He covered his embarrassment by quickly heading into the cabin.

"So, this is the famous Romero summer home." Suave set his bag beside the couch. *"Que chevere!* A little more modern than I expected—oh, look at that. Widescreen TV, a VCR, and everything!"

"Yeah, my dad loves the great outdoors, his style of roughing it—but doing without creature comforts isn't his idea of fun." Her laugh rang with affection. "He would've driven the castaways on 'Gilligan's Island' crazy. *'Oyeme, gente!* Forget that one radio! I want to *see* the Yankees!' "

"Que hombre mas malcreado!" Jestingly, he called her father a spoiled brat. "Let me get those other bags. Be right back in."

"You need any help?"

"No, you relax. It's just a couple of bags."

On the way back from the car, it struck him as sadly familiar. The past was full of that same scene—so everyday and mundane in nature—of transporting supermarket bags from the car to a home. With his arms full, he nudged the door closed with his leg and pushed it shut with his hip.

Need any help, hon? Once it had been Tracy's voice—not Alina's—still honeyed and clear in his memory, preventing one beat of his heart.

Maybe he wasn't ready for this. There was a difference between someone who considered himself prepared for a new romantic relationship and one who dived in heart first. He was disappointed by his own reaction. It was too late to change things now, to say a rushed farewell, and drive back to pick up Ellie and go home. He was there now with Alina, who'd come because the weekend together was *his* idea.

Perhaps it would be okay if things remained strictly platonic, with no sex to entangle them. It was entirely possible for a man and a woman to share the same living quarters for a weekend without acting like hormone-crazed teenagers.

Walking back into the cabin, he saw her sorting through a stack of CDs by the sound system. If worse came to worst, he'd have to be truthful with her. They would have to take it slow if a relationship was to flourish between them. She had lost her husband, so she'd understand that when Tracy died, she'd taken a part of Suave with her. And it was going to take a little longer for him to mend.

"You like India?"

Suave took a break from unpacking the groceries to glance at her.

"Is that a singer or a group?" he asked.

"A singer."

"Sure, why not? I never heard her before."

"Oh, that's right. When it comes to music, you're American. That's okay. You're in for an education in Latin music this weekend."

He accepted the tease goodnaturedly. "There's absolutely no rock music in this whole place?"

"Relax. If you start going through withdrawal, you can dip into the little stash of Eric Clapton and Santana that Quinn forgot to take with him."

As she joined him in the kitchen, his eyes were attracted to the gentle sway of her hips, which had a less than gentle effect on him.

Without being obvious, he watched her move about the kitchen, from the refrigerator to the cabinets, storing items in their proper places. She turned putting away groceries—bending and reaching and tossing her hair over her shoulder— into a sensual banquet for the eyes.

Now he was totally confused. He wasn't ready, but he wanted her. Wanted her so badly that she had him fantasizing about clearing off a space for them both on the butcher block table and—

"Delicious! You read my mind."

He cleared his throat and turned to her. She was holding up a box of devil's food cookies.

"I love these!" she enthused.

"So do I. They have no nutritional value whatsoever, but they're great."

"I'm stealing one now. One for you?"

"Maybe after I check out the rest of the digs. You enjoy them."

To quote Ellie, he wasn't the world's neatest guy. Whenever he went on vacation, it was his daughter with whom he felt perfectly at home being the typical male slob. Suave usually scouted out a corner of a hotel room to toss the suitcases. Right away, Ellie would transfer items into the drawers and closet.

The well-swept house with everything in place led him to the conclusion that he was rooming with another orderly lady. He hauled the bag down the short hallway, discovering a bathroom, a laundry utility closet, and one bedroom. One room had a bed that was considerately left made by its previous occupants.

The Romeros didn't skimp on detail. The dresser drawer he opened was constructed of solid oak—and within it lay a small pile of folded bikini underwear.

Now, *that* was a sight he hadn't seen in a long time. Of course, he'd washed and dried Ellie's clothing, but these items belonged to an adult. He felt heat circulating in his head and other key points in his body.

It's only her underwear!

Fortunately, he composed himself before she peeked through the door.

"I took, um, the left side," she faltered. "And the two bottom drawers."

"Oh. Okay. Fine with me."

"Suave?"

He played it cool, not looking at her as he opened the bag on the bed. "Yeah?"

"Is it just me, or does this feel strange?"

Relaxed by her honesty, he offered a smile. "It feels sorta strange, yeah."

"I . . . don't want us to feel this way all weekend long."

"No. Me, neither."

Silence filled the air between them. Suave sat on the bed, resting his arm across the suitcase. With her hands clasped behind her back, Alina leaned against the doorframe. A trace of sadness and his impending disappointment urged him to reach for an embrace, but he remained seated.

"I'll leave if you want me to. No hard feelings."

"No, that's . . . I could leave, too. You had this place first."

"I can't see you doing that, Alina. I'll leave."

He began to zip up his bag but was stopped by a hand brushing lightly across his arm.

"I don't really want you to leave, Suave. Because I was—I couldn't wait until this day came. It's just now that it's here, I'm afraid."

"Look, if it's any consolation, baby, I'm scared as hell, too."

Beautiful! He had called Alina Romero "baby." But, glancing at her, he detected no objection.

"If we both stay," he assured her, "nothing has to happen here, okay? I don't want you feeling pressured."

"I don't want that, either. I don't want you to think I expect anything."

"All right. And that means—I mean, that *doesn't* mean that I don't want to, either. Because I do."

Alina inched away from the wall. "You do what?"

"I do . . . I do. . . ." Suave shook his head, chuckling. "You've still got it, Alina. Don't ever let anybody tell you you don't."

"I still have what?"

"The thing you had when we were kids that made me dizzy every time I looked at you. You still make me feel like a kid around you, too."

"Really? Well, I got news for you, Suavecito. You *must* have always had what you have now—only, I never noticed it before."

So, the feeling was mutual. Or better yet, the urge to hop into bed and set it on fire was mutual. A hug wouldn't hurt, he decided, gently pulling her closer to him and closing his arms around her. Her arms, winding around his waist, wrapped just as easily around his spirit.

A platonic hug: that was what she was going for, but she failed miserably. What she wanted was another kiss. Another one, longer than the impulsive one in the maze, a kiss created in privacy. If she willed it away, maybe the longing would pass.

The challenge was finding her will, which

seemed to be missing in action. Ending the embrace was a great place to start, assuming that she could force herself to push away from him. He demonstrated more self-discipline in loosening his hold on her.

"I have to finish putting my stuff away," he murmured, huskily. "It's not much."

"Take your time. It's still early. Afterwards, we can go for a swim. Or . . . you know . . . if you want to go off and do something by yourself, that's not a problem."

"Oh, no? I'd say it is. What do I wanna go off by myself for? I came here, hoping to spend time with you."

"Uh-huh. Well, that's what I came here for, too." She pushed strands of hair behind her ear. "And—what was I saying?"

"I have no idea. I'm standing here, and all I'm thinking about is how much I wanna kiss you."

She looked up at him with sweet anticipation. "There's nothing wrong with that. A kiss is just a kiss."

His laugh had a male roughness to it. "This kiss ain't just gonna be a kiss."

"Neither was the first one I got from you. I would hope this one would be as great as that one."

They hadn't even been in the house for an hour yet, and things were already beginning to heat up between them. She'd never live it down. From this day forward, any time they'd see each other the rather wanton attitude of hers would come back to haunt her.

She was having trouble comprehending her own actions. It was as if another part of her were surfacing, eclipsing the person she'd been since Marco died. That secret facet of hers—or not so secret since it existed before—came to life fully as his mouth descended to hers. His lips parted slightly, moistening hers, then parted a bit more, and her tongue sought his.

An imaginary door seemed to open inside her, to emotions and sensations kept under an imaginary lock and key. Before guilt could garner a foothold, Alina gave herself permission to accept another kiss, longer and more possessive than its predecessor, and with it, the permission to enjoy it.

His arms were around her again, and her hands glided up his arms, grasping his shoulders tightly. There was a fun aspect to kissing him there, in the bedroom of the house that was rightfully her parents'. During its construction, she and Marco had been living in Florida. She was the only one of the sisters who hadn't had the opportunity to use it as a romantic hideaway. And by the time she got to, the one sharing it with her was Suave Rivera.

His hand stroked her back slowly. She almost guided his hand to anywhere on her body that he wished to explore.

Kissing. That's enough right now. Unless he wants to . . ., she thought.

But his touch fascinated her. Gently but deliberately, his hand traveled to the nape of her neck, which was veiled by her hair. Between kisses, he paused to smile at her, and his eyes closed as he lowered his face to kiss and taste the skin of her neck. Alina filled her hands with his hair, maneuvering around him to meet his mouth with her own again.

"We're only gonna kiss, right?" Suave asked.

"I don't know. That was the plan." She laughed and then eyed him seriously. "Why? Do you want more?"

"I want more. But that's up to you."

"I don't want it to be up to me. I want whatever's going to happen, to happen."

"All right. But you have to tell me one thing, first."

"What's that?"

He took her face in his hands, raising it to look her in the eye.

"Tell me, right now, if you'll feel uncomfortable around me later. Because if you will, we're stopping now."

Alina looked steadily back at him. She didn't want to lie any more than she wanted him to stop his kisses and caresses.

"I want this with you, and it won't get in the way between us later, as far as I'm concerned. As long as it doesn't make you uncomfortable, either."

Suave murmured something that was lost in a kiss. Reaching behind him, he shoved the bag to the floor, clearing a spot for them on the bed. Then he lowered himself backward onto the mattress, taking her with him.

He knew it was wrong, demanding something from her that was beyond his own reach to guar-

antee. Basically, he didn't fear feeling awkward at
some future gathering at her sister's nearly as
much as Alina's effect on him scared him.

Now, he understood why he'd avoided other
women in his life. He had never been a man who
took relationships lightly, drifting from one
women's bed to the next. That soulless style of
lovemaking held no appeal to him. His experience with women was limited; dates in his youth
were few and far between, since he spent most of
his time pursuing Tracy. He was young when he
married her, and he'd never been unfaithful to
her in all the years they were married.

Although, the bottom line remained: Tracy
loved him, but he'd failed repeatedly to incite her
passion. And he'd accepted it because—because
why? Because he was young and so blindly in love?

And stupid, to accept less?

Alina knelt above him, straddling him. She
pulled her blouse off, revealing a simple white bra
outlining the curve of her breasts. Smiling, she
took both of his hands, placing one on each swell
of flesh that filled his palms. To her pleasure and
his, Suave reached behind her to undo the clasp
and slid the undergarment off her slowly to savor
the view.

It all boiled down to one basic fact: when he
made love to a woman, he didn't check his feelings or heart at the door. He brought both of
those essentials with him to bed as he'd done before—and as he was doing now, with Alina.

Holding her securely by the waist, he rolled on
top of her. Hurriedly, Suave yanked his shirt off

and tossed it aside. He then added his belt to the heap. How she trembled when he kissed her breasts, teasingly circling the areolas with his tongue, was tender and endearing to him.

He could hear her breath coming as hard and fast as his now. He was swept up in touching her, in hearing her little gasps, in the feel and heat of her body. He pulled off his shorts, remembering to take the condom from the pocket, then unzipped hers and peeled them down her bare legs.

If he gave her pleasure, if he showed her they had a chance together, if he proved he was a good, hardworking and loyal man, then what?

Love had taught him a variety of lessons: that a man could make love to a woman, but making her love him was light years beyond his control. That there was such a thing as being *too* selfless. That love really *was* a two-way street. That he deserved the same amount of passion that he offered.

The moment he was inside Alina, he saw that her eyes fully opened and was surprised at the expression reflected in them. Excitement overtook him as he heard her breathless announcement.

"If I knew this was the way you'd make me feel, I would've met you a lot sooner, Suave."

Her body's response confirmed her words. At first tense and stiff, she'd loosened up, moving as best she could under him to increase the exhilaration. He wanted to tell her that he felt the same way, that he would've broken every traffic law to get to that cabin to be with her, but he'd lost his ability to speak. He was swept up in the currents of sensual charge passing between their bodies, making himself slow down at points to prolong the buildup of excitement before the climax.

Each time he slowed down, she delighted and aroused him with feminine groans and brief, earthy laughter. When he sensed neither of them could hold on any longer, he moved more swiftly and sensuously, the crescendo made more intense for him by her hands clutching his shoulders and a quiet but highly sexy cry of ecstasy coming from the back of her throat.

Seven

"*No te digo que este chiquito es candela!* And Justin's having a great time. Quinn handed him a helmet, and we took him dirtbiking up in the mountains. He doesn't miss his Mami at all!"

Alina propped the phone against her ear with her shoulder. "I know you better than that, Mercedes. You wouldn't let my son anywhere near a motorcycle!"

She heard a mischievous giggle on the other end. "No, but Quinn thought about it before I talked him out of it."

"Good. You two will live to see another anniversary together, then. I won't have to kill my brother-in-law."

"No, but seriously, Justin's doing fine. He should be back any minute, too. Quinn took him out to rent some videos, and we're going to have a special kid's dinner."

Smiling, Alina pushed avocado slices onto a plate of red onion strips and sprinkled them with olive oil. "Oh, yeah? What's on the menu?"

"Oh, all fun stuff! *Te lo puedes imaginar.* Tacos, macaroni and cheese, spareribs from the Chinese restaurant, hot wings. And for dessert, ice cream and cake."

"Ah! Cholesterol heaven!"

"True. And it's probably not. . . ." Mercedes hesitated, "what *real* parents would whip up."

"Not on only a daily basis, no. But for a special dinner? Sounds like you and Quinn put a lot of time and effort in it, and Justin's going to love it."

"And how's it going up there?"

She set the dish of avocado and a casserole dish of roasted potatoes onto the table. From the kitchen, she could hear the steaks sizzling on the grill manned by Suave.

"Everything's going pretty well. We're about to sit down to dinner in a few minutes."

Mercedes clicked her tongue. "Well, that's an evasive answer if I've ever heard one."

"I'll tell you all about it when I get home." Clutching the back of a chair, she changed the subject. "So now that you've had a taste of what it's like to have a little one around, are you and Quinn getting psyched to have a baby?"

"We're only finishing out the first day. Ask me again tomorrow night. If I don't pass out from exhaustion before then. Of course I'm teasing. Justin's a lot of fun to have around."

"Well, if he's not too enamored by his aunt and uncle and remembers Mami, have him call me before he goes to bed."

"I will. And he's enamored by us, all right. But every so often, it's 'Mami this' and 'Mami that.' He's having fun—but he misses you, Alina."

The door to the back porch swung open, and Suave walked in with steaks fresh off the grill. Alina rearranged the plates to make room for them.

"Tell him I miss him, too." She caught Suave smiling at her. "And give him a kiss and a hug for me."

"That's what I have to do after dinner," Suave said, sitting down with her at the table. "Call Ellie, see how she's doing. If she remembers me, of course."

"Good luck. I'm a distant memory to Justin."

"He's having a good time with Mercedes and Quinn?"

"Yep. And they're having a good time with him."

"Easier to have fun when there's two of you. One helps out the other, so somebody on the team always has energy."

He'd voiced her silent sentiment. Mercedes's creative kid-style dinner brought back similar memories of years gone by to Alina. She could relate to Suave's comment, knowing what it was like to rush home from work, pick Justin up from her mother-in-law's home, and try to squeeze in quality time between the truckloads of adult and parental responsibilities.

To a single parent, energy was sometimes a precious commodity.

"What're you doing?" she asked, seeing him bowing his head.

"Uh . . . saying grace."

"Grace? Really?" Instinctively, she pulled her hands away from the avocado dish, which she was about to hand to him.

"You don't have to say it. To me, it's like, you know . . . force of habit." Apologetically, he continued, "Not to make you uncomfortable."

"That doesn't make me uncomfortable. I can say it with you." Folding her hands in front of her plate, she closed her eyes, opening one to glance at him. "You're going to say it, though, right?"

"Yeah, but real short and sweet. This is actually Ellie's gig, at home." Bowing his head, he murmured hurriedly, "We thank You for this food and for each other's company, and please take care of our children and bless those watching over them. Amen."

"Amen."

Suave opened his eyes again, immediately looking at Alina. She sat with her hands folded for a few moments, a sublime smile on her face, then reached for the avocado plate and handed it to him. He scooped out a spoonful and set it on her plate, taking another spoonful for himself.

Curiosity tugged at him. "What're you thinking about?"

"About how we never said grace in our house. Not growing up and not in what became my house, later on."

"Well, we didn't, either. I think Ellie was about Justin's age when we started doing it. Tracy found a nice church, close to our neighborhood, and talked me into going with her every Sunday. She said she'd been thinking about it for a long time, how a kid should have a good spiritual foundation, and she wanted that for Ellie."

"And you?"

Suave chuckled. "I did my part. I went to church every Sunday. I left the 'spiritual foundation' part up to the mom in the family. But it's . . . sorta my responsibility now."

Alina marveled inwardly. How little she'd thought of Tracy once, branding her loose and easy for a lifetime. Who would have given the girl credit for becoming a mother who took into account all areas of raising her child, including instilling morals and beliefs in her, adding to that traditions which became part of life's tapestry?

The answer was obvious: Tracy had lacked those things in her own life. As Suave confided earlier, the bad schoolgirl's home life was rough; he didn't expound upon it, yet Alina was capable of filling in the gaps. Tracy wanted to give her daughter more than she'd had in her own life. She didn't want Ellie to grow up and become the school tramp; she wanted to give her idyllic memories of going to the neighborhood church every Sunday with her parents.

"Marco and I also went—on Christmas Eve and Easter and Palm Sunday and all that. The same church where Justin was baptized in Miami."

"Well, that's good."

"Yes, but I think Tracy had the right idea, making it more consistent. She sounds like she was a wonderful mother."

He held a slice of steak poised on his fork, regarding her fondly. "She was."

"And a great wife."

"That, too. There's only one improvement I would've made. But I couldn't, and it was our marriage's one shortcoming."

Alina knew what he was going to say. "You did a terrific job with these steaks, Suave. They're delicious."

He held a rum cooler in his hand, sipping it slowly to wash down his dinner.

"You know, we've talked about everything tonight, except what happened here this afternoon," he reminded her. "And I've been hoping that we could discuss it."

It was stated as a fact, with no pressure or hint of complaint. And he was right. Alina had avoided talking about their lovemaking, which felt as if it had been waiting to happen. The residue of it was still with her, a lingering tingle on every inch of her skin.

Something so simple and ordinary as sitting with him at the same table, a man and a woman sharing a meal, and she'd forgotten how splendid an event it was. The first day at the cabin was winding down, bringing with it a mysterious satisfaction, a reawakening of her senses.

"What is there to discuss?" she asked. "It was incredible."

"It *was*?" Suave cleared his throat. "It was for me. For you, too, then?"

Alina swallowed a bite of roasted potato, repeating with as much fervor as the first time, "For me, it was incredible. And I loved it."

The rest of the meal was eaten in silence, leaving Alina to her own reflections. Suffice to say, Suave wasn't the stereotypical Latino male who was so convinced of his own prowess in bed. In some ways, he reminded her of Suave the boy. How easy it was to confuse "unassuming" with "unsure", to mistake "square peg" with "individual." Maybe the difference could be attributed to the clarity of a woman's vision versus that of a girl.

Yet, there was something else she wanted to discuss. She finished what was left of her avocado slices and approached the subject without temerity.

"Back to what we were saying about beliefs and morals," Alina began. "I don't want you to think that this is something I do all the time—go off on a weekend alone with a man."

Suave's response was calm. "I didn't think that. We already talked about that."

"Yes, but I mean, in general, I don't parade men in and out of Justin's life. Maybe I'm a prude, and I don't—it's not that I'm judging someone who does—"

"Well, I don't see that as being a prude. And I don't judge anybody, either, but parents have a responsibility to their kids—especially kids who've gone through losing the other parent. Emotionally, you can't do that to them, constantly bringing strangers in and out of their lives."

She breathed a sigh of relief. She was so afraid he'd misinterpret what she was saying, of him thinking she was referring to Tracy and becoming offended.

He finished his dinner and leaned toward her slightly, with his arms folded on the table.

"That's it, exactly," she agreed. "And it's not as if I didn't want a—a relationship with anyone, because the thought has crossed my mind. Many times."

"And you always pushed away from it because you thought, 'I already had the best. I'll never find anyone who can hold a candle to him.' Or even better, 'I'm not going to get myself into that situation just because I'm lonely.' "

"You don't want to do anything on the basis of loneliness," she concurred. "But it does . . . it gets lonely."

"Sure, when you don't have an adult to talk to." Suave smiled. "Sometimes, that's all you want. Someone to talk to, heart-to-heart."

"About everything or about nothing." Then she assured him, "But I'm not doing this out of loneliness."

"Uh-huh. Anything wrong with loneliness? Isn't that human, too? Because sometimes, when Ellie's asleep and I'm up late watching whatever movie happens to be on, I get sick of the sound of voices coming out of a box in the living room. But that's all there is to listen to some nights."

And I want to hear footsteps in the next room—lighter footsteps than mine but heavier than Ellie's. Earlier in the evening, Suave heard Alina moving about in the kitchen while he tended the steaks on the grill. He listened to the sounds intently, with the same interest he'd taken when she had been in the shower. Her presence in the cabin naturally beguiled him.

"At least you didn't feel that way," he said, "when you were married, too. Marco probably didn't even have to be around, and he was still with you."

He rose from the table, collecting both of their plates. Alina started to stand, but his hand on her shoulder gently pressed her back down.

"I'll do this. I'll take care of the coffee, too. I get to take it easy at home, with Ellie doing it. You do it all the time. Take a break tonight."

Draining the last few drops of her cooler, Alina asked, "You felt that way, even when Tracy was alive?"

"Not always. It's kinda tough, though, being the only one in love."

"I would think so, sure. Would you have stayed with her, Suave?"

"For the rest of my life." His answer was automatic, dutiful, even to himself. Giving it thought, he set the plates and utensils in the sink. "That's what marriage is, right? Forever. But I don't know. Marriage is also supposed to be shared by two people in love with each other. Okay, the honeymoon doesn't go on and on, but being in love is supposed to take on new meaning, right?"

"It becomes deeper than fireworks."

"That's what I want." Searching through the cabinets, he found a can of El Pico coffee and set it on the counter, then turned to her. "I would've probably stayed with Tracy. But now that she's gone, there's no way I'd put myself through that a second time. I want a woman to be in love with me, as much as I am with her."

"That's the way it should be." This time, Alina did stand up, pushing both chairs into the table. "It's a beautiful night. You want to have our coffee out in the back?"

Is that the end of the discussion? Suave hid his confusion behind a lighthearted attitude.

"Yeah, let's do that."

"Good! Give me a few minutes to get a couple of things, and meet me out there."

Suave knew that dropping the mention of love too quickly in their conversation had sent her hunting for an excuse out of the kitchen. Alina must've figured that, given some space, the discussion would cool off a bit and become easier to handle.

He paused as he made the espresso in the old-fashioned *cafetera*. He scolded himself for reading too much into one little action. That was a fault of his—not only with Alina but also with Tracy at the beginning of their marriage. The two seldom fought; their arguments were more disagreements than the shouting matches some couples engaged in.

However, there had been one time, during the second or third year of their marriage, when he'd allowed an assumption to almost ruin everything. Ellie was a baby then, too young to remember. Their family had fallen on hard times financially, with Suave temporarily laid off from his job and working for a small printing outfit under the table. To compensate, Tracy had taken a job as a receptionist at a lawyer's downtown office, leaving Ellie with an elderly neighbor.

Suave had met Tracy's boss on one occasion. Her boss was young, cocky, and good-looking— *very* good-looking. A guy with cash to burn who appeared just a bit too friendly with his new employee.

He'd told himself that it was stupid to worry, that he trusted Tracy from one end of the Earth to the other. Until he had called her office one day to tell her he'd be working late that night, and he was told that Tracy had called in sick. A call to the baby-sitter confirmed his suspicions—Tracy hadn't picked Ellie up. He'd called their apartment and reached the answering machine. As a final attempt, he'd called her doctor, who hadn't seen or heard from Tracy that day—and then Suave jumped head-first into a conclusion.

His pretty wife wasn't at work, home, the doctor's, or the baby-sitter's. This lead him to believe that the only place she *could* be was in the arms of that money-flashing lawyer.

He stopped thinking for a moment and looked out the window. He saw Alina out in the backyard. She'd gone through the front door and around the house, perhaps for the sake of surprising him. With her back turned, she covered the picnic table with a tablecloth and placed an oil lantern in the center. Once lit, the flame illuminated the table.

Suave smiled, then heard coffee bubbling out of the *cafetera*'s spout behind him. Before it could splatter on the stove, he shut off the burner.

What happened that day with Tracy was out of character for him. After telling his boss that he had a family emergency, he drove home like a maniac. She wouldn't be there, he assumed; she'd be off somewhere else, in her boss' apartment or in a ritzy Vegas hotel.

The idea in going home was to leave no stone unturned, to wipe out any excuse Tracy could use. Suave had looked for her everywhere, and she was nowhere to be found because, quite simply, she'd cheated on him. She'd broken her wedding vows and left him for a dalliance with another man.

The memory of that day still made him wince. He poured espresso into the demitasse cups, remembering he'd been almost crazy when he burst through the apartment's door—startling Tracy in the bedroom. In her robe, pale, and with her hair tied up. She'd started to go to work that morning but had turned around, ill with a twenty-four hour bug going around the office. She'd left Ellie at the babysitter to rest and let the machine answer any calls.

She had demanded, "Where did you think I was, Brendan?"

Any time Tracy called him "Brendan" instead of "Suave," he knew a storm was on its way. She knew too well that his suspicions originated from her less-than-chaste past. After all she'd done to prove that she'd changed, she lashed out at him through the hurt.

You jealous jerk! If you can't trust me, there's the door. I'm not the person I used to be.

She'd ordered him out of the apartment. Suave had complied, making a show of slamming the door—and then he heard the deadbolt lock into place. Infuriated, he returned to a miserable day at work, believing he'd lost his family.

With nowhere to go afterward, he called her from a friend's house and swallowed his pride, apologizing for the insinuation and asking her to take him back. Tracy broke down on the phone, and so did he.

I want you to come home, but I want you to know how much you hurt me. I thought you knew me better than that, Suave.

He was so far from that night now, balancing two demitasse cups as he walked off the porch to join Alina at the picnic table under the stars.

In Alina's eyes, he could see something he'd never seen in Tracy in all the years they were together—desire. Not true love, because that took time to flourish—but the possibility was there.

And if it wasn't, if he was mistaken, then he needed to know. Being in another man's shadow—Marco's—wouldn't suffice, either. This time, love had to be balanced, or it was better to be alone.

Loud and urgent, a siren thrust Alina out of her dream and back into reality. It was a disjointed dream, more like a collection of old but vibrant photos than a coherent nightscape story.

Pictures of what? And why was she in a strange bed? Something warmed her around her waist, and breathing brushed her shoulder softly. It was Suave, snuggled around her in his sleep. Now she remembered: She was in the cabin, not at home or at high school.

Why high school? Ever since she'd gone to a college seminar on the interpretation of dreams, she'd kept a small notebook and a pen by her bed to record her dreams and try to figure out what they meant. Some dreams were like movies and were even entertaining. Others were like an obscure set of pictures, clumsily hashed together, sometimes involving the senses besides just the eyes of the unconscious.

This one had featured a fire engine siren, the only thing that stood out. That wasn't unusual. For years after Marco's death, the common occurrence of hearing a police or fire siren blaring through the streets brought the image of his face—as if the sound was, in some eerie way, a familiar song.

Fire in the school. If she was very still and cleared her mind, sometimes a few of the dream-pictures would drift back. One was of herself at her current age but wearing a cheerleading uniform, complete with tassles swinging from short, white boots. Another fragment involved smoke at each end of a corridor. The school was empty, except for her and her Spanish teacher, Mrs. Prieto, an older lady who died a year or so after Alina's graduation.

Alina eased out from under Suave's embrace.

She started to get out of the bed but stopped, gazing at him.

He had been in the dream, too. At least she remembered seeing a picture of him, though he was younger. Now it came back: She and Suave trying to persuade Mrs. Prieto to escape from the school, which was burning down.

And I thought I started the fire. I started it, and I was crying because I was in so much trouble. I was afraid they were going to catch me, and I was so ashamed.

She propped her pillow against the headboard and laughed. To imagine herself, the captain of the cheerleading squad, as an amateur arsonist was initially hilarious.

She hadn't seen Marco, but that wasn't strange. Alina had dreamed of him only once, months after he'd died. She had awakened from that dream wishing they could last longer than nature dictated.

In the dream, Marco was handsome and healthy—exactly as he looked before the aneurism killed him. She had walked into the bedroom to find him dressing in a suit, standing in front of the mirror while buttoning the cuffs of his sleeves.

"Alina, you're not even dressed," the dream-Marco had chided her. "We're going to be late for dinner."

That was so like him! He hated to be late for any event. But Alina hadn't budged, afraid to approach him. "Marco, I thought you died."

"Me? I died? No." He slipped a tie over his collar. "I'm still alive."

The dream ended there. It was almost as if he never had to step foot in her dreams again, never had to intrude upon them, because he'd accomplished his purpose—to console her with the notion that love couldn't be buried in the ground, that it habitually cheated death with its power.

Suave stirred beside her, laying his arm on her thigh. Last night, they hadn't made love before going to sleep. Neither had wanted to pressure the other for sex. The temperature in the mountains had cooled slightly overnight, and it was she who suggested they simply hold each other and fall asleep in each other's arms.

Ironically, it had still felt like making love. In his arms, she felt the same jubilation, the same intimacy as earlier, when they'd explored each other sexually.

It was a wish come true, a silent wish she'd denied herself. So many times she'd wanted just to be held in a pair of strong arms. All she'd wanted was genuine tenderness, which made for a sweet and delicious bed waiting for her.

Suave had answered that wish, easily, without even trying.

I set fire to the school. I was shaking Mrs. Prieto, shouting at her to come with us.

Tamara was in the same school, yet not in the dream, either. Missing, too, was Tracy. No Ellie, no Justin. The only ones she'd seen in the dream were the Spanish teacher, Suave, and herself.

She slipped out of bed, careful not to wake him, and headed to the shower. The last piece of the puzzle slid into place after the final picture re-visited her memory—of the delicate teacher who obstinately refused to leave the presence of danger, looking up at Alina, kindly.

So, you were the one who started the fire. Why should you be ashamed of that, my dear?

Eight

Shaded under a tree and lying on a blanket, Alina looked absolutely beautiful. The only make-up she'd bothered to apply that day was a layer of lipstick, most of which had faded. Lying there, peacefully reading a book, she made Suave want to haul the boat to the shore and make love to her again.

Suave sighed, giving his fishing line more slack, then reeling it in again. That morning, they'd driven into town, had a big breakfast at a local diner, and had spent another hour browsing through antique shops.

Upon their return, he hadn't been in the mood to take the rowboat out on the lake to fish, when staying near the cabin with his lovely roommate was so enticing.

Yet, what they both needed was a little space. They still had the rest of the afternoon and the evening and part of Sunday before heading home. Suave thought it wise to avoid even the slightest chance of cabin fever by allowing a few minutes to read or hike or do whatever she wished.

Suave had spent an hour on the lake consulting his watch and casting glances back toward shore. Alina would also look up from her book now and then. She didn't make it too obvious, panning the lake with her eyes, which had the tendency to linger on him when she thought he wasn't looking.

Things were going so well—too well, in fact. But a weekend was just that—two days out of an entire week, or more aptly, out of their entire lives. How was he supposed to go back to life as it was before once they closed up the cabin and left for home?

She looked up again. She decided to forego the diversion and looked straight at him. To his surprise, she puckered her lips and blew him an exaggerated kiss.

Suave grinned at her and bellowed, "Hey, you! Tell your father there ain't no fish in here!"

"Diego said he caught quite a few fish in there!" she shouted back.

"Yeah? Well, I think Diego is spinning his tall tales again!" He watched as she knelt on the blanket, setting the book on her lap. "What're you reading, anyway?"

"The reading material in that cabin is kinda limited! It was between this book, Mami's *Buenhogar* magazines, or an erotic thriller somebody left behind!"

"Oh. An *erotic* thriller. Does *that* make it more thrilling?" He could see her smile and shaking her head. "So what're you reading?"

"*By Reason of Insanity* by G. Miki Hayden! A mystery. It's really good. There was also a *True Confessions* magazine. Must be Mercedes' because she loved those. I guess she doesn't have to hide them from Mami anymore!"

It was crazy, carrying on a conversation across a lake. Suave reeled in the line fully, tucked the rod into the boat, and started rowing toward shore. He'd had enough of fishing in a fishless lake.

"Sure, it had to be one of those two trouble-makers, Mercedes or Tamara!" he yelled back. "I bet a good girl like you never bought a magazine she had to hide from her mother."

The good-natured lilt was still in her voice, but she frowned. "I wasn't *that* good! I did some crazy things."

"Oh, yeah, sure you did! Like maybe you . . . purposely forgot to pay a fine on an overdue library book or something equally innocent like that."

"Excuse me?"

Chuckling, he advised himself to stop. He got out of the boat and dragged it onto the shore.

"Is that my sister's version of my life you're spouting?" Alina asked. Now that he was closer, their voices returned to a normal volume. "I'm sure Tamara made me look like some geeky Goody Two-shoes."

"No, *neña,* not Goody Two-shoes. To hear her tell it, I always thought she was the Dominican-Cuban version of Jan Brady from 'The Brady Bunch.' And you were . . . Marcia!"

She fought back a laugh and made room for him on the blanket.

"I got drunk," she said to prove her point. "Once."

Suave gasped, dramatically. "You *didn't?*"

"Yes, I did. In college. Somebody put liquor into the punch at this party, and I didn't realize it, so I kept getting more punch. By the end of the party, they had to carry me out of there."

"Ah, but you see, that is *accidentally* getting drunk. Accidentally being three sheets to the wind doesn't count."

She closed her book and put it aside, determined to impress him. "All right. Try this one on for size. This happened to me in college, too—"

"College really corrupted you, huh? That's 'higher education' for you."

"*Ya, chico, escucha!* Tamara doesn't know this. My parents don't know about it, either."

"And you don't want me to tell them, right?"

Alina ignored his teasing. "And you didn't notice it—um, last night, because—because you weren't looking for it."

Now he was curious. "What happened?"

"I was trying to get into this sorority. I don't know why. I didn't even like half the girls in it, but it was like *the* sorority to hail from in school. So, they put you through all these stupid tests, or rites, whatever they call them. And the last rite was that you had to get a tattoo of their mascot."

"A tattoo? You have a tattoo? My next logical question is, where?"

"I bet Tamara doesn't have one."

"No, but Tracy did. She got it after high school,

in Vegas, after we were married." He pointed to a spot on his chest. "Right over her left breast, this tiny rose."

"That actually sounds pretty. But she wanted to get it. I didn't want mine, but I did it anyway. I wasn't raised to think a girl should have a tat-too—"

"Because nice girls didn't get tattoos." He smiled. No accusation, no offense taken. "So, where is it? And *what* is it? And how come you didn't show it to me last night?"

"Because I'm not all that proud of it. It was this crazy—*bad* thing that I did." She beamed. "And that was just the beginning. I drove a bunch of the girls one night and ran right through a red light, and this cop caught me."

"And he probably gave you this tough-guy lec-ture, but he didn't give you a ticket, anyway."

"How did you know?"

"Because you're a pretty girl!" Suave lifted her chin with one hand. "Cops rarely give tickets to pretty girls. Don't you know that? Now, with guys, it's tough luck. Me, he would've busted out a hun-dred-dollar ticket, plus ran me down to the sta-tion for good measure."

Alina fidgeted with the tie string on her dress. "But you've never been arrested?"

"No. I've been to jail, but as a visitor."

"You were? Who were you visiting?"

"Tracy's dad. He did some time in Big Spring, in Texas, for dealing heroin."

The mood grew somber. Licking her lips, Alina asked, "Is he out now?"

"Yeah, he's been out for some years now. We didn't hear from him anymore, though, so I don't know how he's doing. It was kind of ironic, because the most time Tracy ever got to spend with him was those few times we drove out to Texas to see him." On a lighter note, Suave smiled. "So you beat a traffic ticket, got a tattoo, and got smashed at a frat party. Any more of the true confessions of Alina Romero?"

She stretched out on the blanket again, getting comfortable, and looked up at him.

"Here you are, comparing me to *La Virgen de la Caridad*. But you're no better. Tamara calls you the original Boy Scout, so that must mean you're squeaky clean, too."

He stretched out, closer to her. "Well, Tamara doesn't know this. And neither do your parents, so I'd appreciate you not telling them."

Alina laughed. "This is going to be good!"

Unable to resist any longer, he gave into the urge to touch her, stroking her hair over one soft shoulder.

"I punched this kid out in sophomore year."

"Really? You?"

"Yeah, I know. I'm a lover, not a fighter. But he pushed me too far, and I just turned around and decked him."

"Did he say something to Tracy?"

"No, he said it to me. I would've plastered him to the wall if he'd said anything about Tracy to my face. But he got off easy with a fat lip."

"What did he say that made you so angry?"

"He called me 'white boy.'" Suave snorted.

"This Latino kid, on my own team. He resented me for playing b-ball better than he did, so he'd call me that every so often. I finally turned around and popped him one in the mouth. And I told him, 'yeah, I'm Irish, and I'm proud. But I'm also as Puerto Rican as you are, and I'm proud of that, too. So next time, you sure as hell better not forget it.' "

Alina's expression was of open admiration. "Good for you!"

" 'Course the coach didn't know what was going on, so he benched us both for fighting. And that was about as nasty as I ever got. So, let's get back to business. Where's this tattoo?"

"You have a one-track mind, Suave!"

"I'm not leaving without seeing it."

Without further ado, she tugged at her dress. His eyes watched the hem rise up her bare calves, traveling up the back of her curvy thighs. It was a spontaneous little striptease, titillating him as the dress rose over the top of her pink bikini underwear.

Alina was quite the vixen. Smirking mischievously at him, she hooked a forefinger through the left side of her underwear and peeled them down, slowly. Emblazoned on her left buttock was a tattoo, slightly over an inch long, colorful and perfectly detailed.

Suave adjusted his glasses for a closer look. "What kind of animal is that?"

"It's a jaguar. You know. It was our mascot."

"Uh-huh. Well, that's one fine-lookin' school spirit."

"Oh, shut up!" She snapped the bikini's elastic back up and flicked down her skirt. "Case closed. I win. I'm badder than you thought I was."

He wasn't letting her off the hook that easily. "Na, that's not gonna cut it. You were *pressured* into doing that."

She rose to her feet, pushing the book aside with her bare toe.

"Yeah, and now I gotta go through life with a wild animal on my butt. Doesn't that count? That I have to live with the consequences of crazy youth?"

"Well, okay, the jury's still out on that. Only because you haven't gotten rid of it, all these years later. You *can* have it removed, you know."

"Oh, I know. I've thought about it. Just haven't done it because . . . I kinda like it."

Suave did a doubletake, chuckling. "For what it's worth, so do I."

"And just to prove my sister—Jan Brady—wrong, once and for all, I'm going to do something I bet none of them has ever done up here, because they're afraid someone will drive by and see them."

"What're you gonna do?"

"Something you've probably never done, either. I'd like to see if you have the nerve to do it."

Cars didn't pass by very often, but they passed often enough. Tamara *was* right—Alina was always the good, upstanding girl, obedient to her parents and teachers and superiors, always following the rules.

On the other hand, this *was* private property, hidden in the mountains where some privacy was assured. She reached under her dress and let her underwear slide down her legs, stepping out of them and leaving them on the blanket.

"Whoa, hold it—are you gonna do what I think you're gonna do?" Suave scrambled to his feet.

"I knew you wouldn't have the nerve," she taunted him playfully.

She crisscrossed her arms, grasping the dress and pulling it over her head. She kept one leery eye on the road: fortunately, there wasn't a car in sight.

Suave kept both eyes on her, not permitting himself to blink. Here was a completely nude, beautiful woman out in the open, appealing to his sense of fantasy and most definitely to his appetite for the sensual, which was now going haywire.

"Who says I don't have the nerve?" he said, pulling off his shirt.

"Good. Because one of the things I came up here for was to swim. Even better if you joined me."

Alina didn't wait for him and walked to the water's edge. Her spectacular, tiny jaguar did the most captivating dance on its sexy canvas—a dance especially for him.

"How many people did you say own houses up here?" Over his shoulder, he consulted the quiet road. He stripped off his belt and unzipped his shorts, bringing them down with his briefs.

"You'd have to ask my dad. I really don't know. It's my first time up at this place, remember?" She tested the water with her toe, finding the temperature formidable but wading further in. "Being this is my first time, I really want to make a splash."

"No kidding. To any parents who are passing by with the kiddies, this house is *not* rated G!" He trotted into the water after her, lifting and lowering his legs heavily to spray the backs of her legs. "How's that for a splash?"

Alina turned and swiftly kicked water at him. Suave growled and chased her, catching her in waist-high water. He picked her up by her hips and dunked her, thinking he'd won the round.

But Alina failed to rise to the surface after a few seconds. With growing concern, he bent over and ran his arms along the area where she had been. Then, he felt something yank hard at his legs, and he fell backward into the murky water.

They emerged together, with Alina's cunning proving a match for his brawn.

"Just when you thought it was safe to go back in the water," she drawled.

Suave wiped his eyes with his hands to get a good look at her. She was wet and glistening from her head to her waist, her long hair straight and shining behind her. The sunlight sparkled on the tiny rivulets of water trailing down her firm breasts. The water hid the rest of her, adding to her mystery. He glided toward her and grabbed her her hips, guiding her body to his.

"Sometimes, of course, you don't care if it's safe," Alina said. "You just have to jump in."

"Yeah. That's what it's like." He signaled his agreement by giving her a burning kiss.

God, touching you is a rush by itself, he thought. It was pure excitement holding her, kissing her. Alina's arms circled his waist and tightened. The texture of her erect nipples against his chest drove him crazy. Her body spoke to him—with its movements, its responses, its heat.

In all its feminine wonder, it made him desire her more. He opened his eyes as the kiss ended, searching the look in her eyes and finding something that made his heartbeat race.

Passion was staring back at him. How did he live without it before? Never seeing it again would be unbearable. Alina brought her mouth to his mouth as her hands swept under the water and clasped his erection, caressing him slowly and deliberately. He placed his hand over hers, bending his knees to enter her.

"No, no," she whispered. "When we get back to the house. I want this to be for you."

"But what about you?"

"Later. In the house. I want this to be something you think about when I'm not there." She sucked in a shaky breath. "Suave, I don't want this to end with the weekend."

He relaxed with his arms around her, enjoying the rippling sensations her hands were creating.

"I don't want it to end, either, Alina," he admitted.

"I haven't wanted anyone the way I want you, not in a long time. I don't know how you feel, but—"

"You know how I feel. You have to. I didn't know what was going to happen when we both came here, but now I can't go back to the way things were, either. Alina. . . ."

"When we get to the house, Suavecito. We'll talk when we get back to the house." The fact that she was so at home with his body confirmed that this was right. His body tensed as the tide of fulfillment came, and he held her against him, his breath fast and warm against the skin of her shoulder. His excitement only served to heighten her own anticipation, knowing that they would be making love shortly back at the house.

And I can't wait for that, she thought.

Suave Rivera had crossed the line from her Tamara's friend to the desire of Alina's heart.

Open in case of emergency. Well, it was time for the best of emergencies.

Fresh from the shower, Alina sat on the edge of the bathtub to unwrap the gift from her sister. Suave would be back at the cabin any minute. She listened for the sound of his car pulling into the driveway. It didn't matter that the lake hadn't yielded a fresh fish dinner because he had driven back to town to pick up some crab legs for them. A delicious dinner like that would beat anything out of the mountain lake.

She tore off the paper, clicking her tongue and giggling at Tamara's sense of humor. Her sister's idea of emergency provisions came in a Victoria's Secret box. With anticipation, Alina shook the top of the box free from the bottom.

Black satin and lace were folded carefully beneath a small card. Its envelope read, PARA MI HERMANA, ALINA. The message made her chest tighten with emotion. HERE'S SOMETHING MAYBE YOU WOULDN'T BUY FOR YOURSELF. YOU'LL LOOK SO BEAUTIFUL IN IT! CON CARINO, TAMARA.

Not Mercedes, not her mother, but Tamarita. The sibling rivalry had died, and in its place was a friendship of her own blood.

She couldn't wait to put it on. But, she was self-conscious, too. Alina had always fallen in between her sisters: not as full-figured as Mercedes, nor as fit and trim as Tamara.

Ah, well. Lingerie has magical powers, doesn't it?

No one could accuse her of not taking care of herself. Maybe she wasn't as tight in some areas as she used to be, but her figure was still pretty decent. Besides, it was a little late for a silly bout with modesty, wasn't it? Suave had already seen everything there was to see—or hide—that weekend.

As soon as she had put the teddy on, she knew her worry was over nothing. It was her size, flowing over her as smoothly as rainwater. The sheer fabric gave a peek at her skin, and its texture was luxurious after a day spent in cotton.

Hearing Suave's car outside, Alina grabbed a brush from the vanity and ran it through her long tresses. She then applied a fresh coat of lipstick, feeling sentimental.

Because . . . why? Because she hadn't looked at herself in a mirror for so long and seen someone other a mother and lover left behind, someone who was a woman. It would be nonsense to imply she'd forgotten that part of herself. It was more like being dormant, put up on a shelf somewhere, as one would do to a dusty heirloom.

She'd started the fire in her dream? It was hard to tell. Suave might've been the real culprit, but it was irrelevant.

A trace of fear remained but not the guilt, which was ridiculous. She wasn't being unfaithful to Marco. Her husband was once a fine boy who'd grown into a good man. Their life together should have lasted longer. And in a way, she'd unconsciously chosen to set herself aside, devoting herself to her son.

Ultimately, that course of action wouldn't have benefited either Justin or herself. Life had already plotted all of the roles she'd play through various stages of her life: the obedient daughter who strove for her parents' approval; the loving and dedicated wife, mother, and teacher; the loyal sister and friend to her two younger siblings.

Now, this was one role that caught her by surprise: *romantic lover.* Would it lead to another role eventually? One that traditionally bore a bad reputation?

Stepmother. I'd like you to meet my dad's second wife, my stepmother, Alina. Or, That's my stepmother—she's such a witch!

Wasn't she getting a little ahead of herself? The front door opened and closed, and she heard Suave's footsteps announcing his return.

"Alina! Wait till you see the dinner we're having! Where are you?"

She pattered into the bedroom.

"I'm in here, Suave!"

It could happen. It would take time, and that was natural. But it wouldn't be that simple. Marriage wasn't a consideration yet; they had both come further in starting a relationship than either one thought possible. Justin was a little guy, able to adapt more easily—but Ellie? Ellie was a preteen, at that delicate age. From what Suave had told Alina, she'd adored her mother and was used to the concept of "Me and Daddy against the world."

"You have to see these crab legs! I got some shrimp for us, too. We just have to—oh. . . ."

He halted at the bedroom door, taking her in.

"Forget the seafood," he mumbled, stepping farther into the room. "Dinner can wait."

"I think so, too."

She liked the way his hands made themselves at home on her waist, closing in the space between them for a kiss. This was going to be better than the first time, because they were shedding what they'd been to each other in the past, becoming new to each other and yet sweetly familiar.

"You look . . . really, really sexy."

Alina accepted the compliment with a bubbly chuckle.

"You got that for me? For this weekend?"

"Um . . . well, no. It was a gift, to be opened in case of an emergency. The emergency is that you made me want to put it on for you."

"Ah. *Me gusta eso!*"

"I thought you would like it." She wiped lipstick off his mouth. "Before anything, I wanted to talk to you."

"Baby, it's gonna be really hard to talk when what I want to do is have you."

"Only one thing I have to know. Because I'm never going to look at you the same way again, after this."

"I've *been* seeing you differently, ever since the maze." Suave saw that she was having trouble expressing herself, and tried to make it easier for her. "I asked you to come here because I wanted us to start fresh. Whatever happened when we were in high school, that's not fresh. This was a place to begin."

"That's what I wanted to know. I feel that . . . that what started here, I want more of. I want more of *you.*" She smiled nervously. "I don't know if I'm ready to take it very fast—"

"We don't have to, Alina. I'm not in a hurry, either." He searched her eyes before continuing, "But I wanna be your man."

"Oh." A joyous laugh burst from her. "I'd love that, Suave, because I'm already falling in love with you."

As she embraced him, Suave held her as close to himself as he could, letting her words have their full impact on him. It felt like he held more woman in his arms than ever before.

Nine

On a sweltering August afternoon, the house closing took place in the air-conditioned office of Guadelupe Ginart, Esq. Lupe, a young and hip Cuban woman who'd handled the closing on Diego and Tamara's property, shuffled papers across the long conference table to her client. As Alina's pen swirled, her father stroked her shoulder, reassuringly.

"Sign that one," the raven-haired attorney said, passing over the next legal document. "And right there on that line, too. Now this one. . . ."

Alina had the sinking feeling she was signing her life away. There was no turning back now, with her real estate agent, Shauna Hodges, at one end of the table and the seller's lawyer at the other. She had nothing in her stomach except two cups of coffee, and she felt queasy.

It was also the first time she'd met Rusty and Merilee Dwyer, the home's previous owners. They made a very cute, gray-haired pair, holding hands like sweethearts through most of the closing. Rusty was a handsome seventy-year-old who'd taken an instant liking to the vivacious Alejandro

Romero. The two chattered on and on about Alejandro's homeland, where Rusty was stationed at Guantanamo as a young man in the service.

Lupe smiled sympathetically at Alina. "Just a couple more to go, and we're done here."

At the lawyer's right hand was a check from the mortgage company in the full amount of the sale price—with an awful lot of zeroes. And to think, she'd get to spend the next thirty years of her life paying it off.

It was scary for her—and it was thrilling. Plans were in place for her to move into the new house that weekend. Mami, always the tough Latina lady, didn't want anyone feeling left out. She called her daughters and left each one an identical message: "You and your sweet *marido* are moving your sister and nephew into their house this weekend. We'll see you then." The one volunteer was Suave. He'd offered his services to help move and promised to bring Ellie along for the ride. Alina accepted, pleased that he'd be there. She didn't have that much furniture; between Diego and Quinn, they could handle it themselves.

Yet in the two weeks that had passed since their weekend together, she and Suave had made time for each other. She'd met him for lunch at work twice, and if he worked late, Suave would call her at night and talk for an hour or more.

They'd discussed getting together with the kids more often. Giving Justin and Ellie a chance to get to know each other would hopefully make the transition as natural as possible for them.

"That's it," Lupe said. She gathered the documents together. "We're done."

"That can't be it," Alina jested. "Don't you want me to use up all the ink in this pen, signing every paper from here to eternity?"

The woman laughed. "That's what it feels like, doesn't it? But, no. We're finished. Mr. Van Druten—this is for your clients."

Alejandro squeezed Alina's shoulder as the check was passed across the table to the other lawyer, a bearded yuppie type. Rusty Dwyer slipped his hand into his suit jacket's pocket.

"And this is for you, young lady," he said in his big, friendly voice. "I hope you and your son will be as happy as my family and I were."

Alina reached across the table for the keys to her new home. "Thank you, Mr. Dwyer."

"You're welcome. And please, call me Rusty. I gave your dad our number, so you can call me if you have any questions about the house, anything at all you want to know."

"Okay, Rusty. Thanks very much."

After almost two hours in that office, Alina was back in her own car, with her father in the passenger seat.

"*Perfecto!*" he commented. "Great timing. You move into the house this week, start the new job in two more weeks, and everything settles into place." He made it sound so easy.

"I'd feel better if everything wasn't happening so close together, you know, Papi?"

Alejandro scoffed. "Ah, things are not happening too close to each other, no." After thinking about it, he shrugged. "Okay, you are right. Everything is happening so damn fast. But this is no problem for you. You are strong."

"Hmmm. You have too much confidence in me, Papi."

"I have a lot of confidence in all of my women. Eh—that is you, your sisters, and your mother."

"Yeah, that better be the women you're talking about—or Mami will strangle you!" She laughed with him. "If it's all right with you, Papi, I'm going to pass by the house. *My* house. Mine and Justin's."

"And the house of whoever else may live there with you someday."

Alina sighed. "Well, we're not talking about marriage yet, Papi."

"That doesn't mean it will never come up in conversation."

"Please. Don't rush me. I can only handle three things at once!" More seriously, she added, "You meant that before, what you said? About that you have confidence in me?"

"Of course. I shouldn't have to say it. You should know this already."

They were only half a mile from the new house now, passing the bait and tackle shops, the diners that dated back to the fifties, and several mini-malls. Alina turned down the radio.

"It means a lot to me to hear you say it. Especially because there were a lot of times, Papi, after

Marco was gone, that oh—I really didn't have confidence in myself. I didn't know what I was going to do, how I was going to raise Justin by myself. If I was even going to make it."

"Well, I know that was the time you were most afraid in your life, *mi cielo*. But our family is always there for each other."

"Yes, but there are times in your life when your family can't be there. As much as they want to, it has to be you, pulling through for yourself and a little child who depends on you. . . ." She paused. "And the years pass, and you're still there, in the struggle, but you're not so afraid any more that you can't celebrate the happiness that comes to you, because you've earned it."

She parked the car along the curb in front of the house and turned to her father. Alejandro was smiling at her, his head tilted. He clutched her hand.

"Come," he said, "let's go look at my daughter's house."

She envisioned how lovely it would look in the fall, when the trees in the front yard changed color and covered the walkway with an autumnal carpet. Not far away, the ocean salted the breeze with its scent. Her father stood with his arm around her, nodding his approval.

"That is a very fine house, Alina," he declared.

I'm in the market for a house, too, and this one would do fine. She remembered Suave's words to the real estate agent, when he'd taken Diego's place to accompany Alina on the second tour through the house. She thought about both him and Ellie as she stood outside her new home, and it occurred to her that it was roomy enough to accommodate the four of them.

Not in the sense of living together; it was too early in the game for that, and besides, Alina was an old-fashioned girl. She had lived with a man as his wife, the first time around, and she would live with Suave as her husband, if the relationship progressed in that direction.

That she even entertained the thought of marrying again—specifically marrying Suave—gave her heart another reason to celebrate.

"You're right, Papi. It is a fine house. But then again"—she nudged his arm—"you're always right!"

On Saturday morning, bright and early, Diego Santamaria and Quinn Scarborough were ready for action. Wearing shorts and short-sleeved shirts to combat the brutal heat forecasted for later in the day, they showed up with their wives at Alina's doorstep and set to work on moving her belongings after a brief conversation over coffee.

Unfortunately for the men, Carmela Romero was another early riser. She was supposed to keep Justin from getting underfoot, although it wasn't necessary. With his grandmother as a self-proclaimed moving supervisor, Justin wasn't the one getting in Diego and Quinn's hair.

"*Digo que no, Quinn!*" she instructed the young

men, who were positioning Alina's couch to move it out the door. "Turn it the other way. That's it, Diego, show him what I mean!"

When Carmela turned to speak with Tamara, Diego raised his eyebrows at Alina, as if to say, *Is this what we have to put up with all day?*

Alejandro had pity on his sons-in-law, defending them from the doorway to the kitchen. *"Concho, mamita, deja que los muchachos lo hagan, ya!* Let them work, Carmela."

"Well, they're doing it wrong, and *you* are doing nothing to direct them!" She pointed at Diego. "No, no, you were carrying it right the first time. Now you are both carrying it wrong!"

"Carmela, it's okay," Quinn said respectfully setting the couch down to address her. He was doing his best to summon patience.

"Oh, you won't think it's okay when it falls on your foot and it breaks!"

"When *what* breaks? My foot or the couch?"

"Both!"

"That's not gonna happen, Carmela—"

"Ay, concho, pero ella no me hace caso!" Alejandro lamented with a hand slapping his side. *"Carmela, por favor, deja los muchachos! No chivas mas!"*

"Oye, no me grites!" His wife, still an attractive spitfire, didn't back down to his rising voice. *"Y el que esta chivando eres tu!"*

There were too many people in that small apartment, Alina decided. That was the problem. She was ready to steer her mother out into the hallway to persuade her to relax, but Mercedes stepped in first. She took Justin by the hand and Carmela by the elbow.

"Sweetie, why don't you, me, and Abuela go look at that cool truck outside?" she asked. "We'll let your uncles work in here, okay?"

Carmela opened her mouth to protest, then allowed Mercedes to lead them out. Alejandro followed, muttering loudly in Spanish about his wife not knowing when to quit. In the hallway, he received a spicy rebuttal from his usually adoring wife.

Quinn slapped his hands together. "Okay, enough fun. Let's get to work. Grab the couch on your end, and whatever you do, don't drop it on my foot. I'd really hate to tell her she was right and I was wrong."

Diego bent over, secured a good grip on the couch, and brought his end up. "I love them, but those two are so tempestuous."

"You're telling me. Growing up, it was like living with a Cuban Spencer Tracy and a Dominican Katherine Hepburn," Alina told him. "I think they love bickering. And they're just as tempestuous when they make up, so it balances out."

Tamara stood near the door, gathering the lighter moving boxes together in one corner.

"When is Suave getting here?" she asked Alina.

"He called and said he was running a little late. He should be here in a few minutes."

"Ahh, Suave." Diego smirked, tilting the couch to get it through the doorway. "Carmela's next victim."

"Hey, I heard that!" Tamara lightly slapped the back of her husband's head, laughing. *"Fresco!"*

Alina smiled at the flirtatious wink Diego flashed at Tamara before she disappeared into the hallway, warmed by the interaction between them. She'd seen those same romantic games between Mercedes and Quinn, and remembered the playful moments during her weekend with Suave.

Now that she knew he was coming over that morning, she couldn't wait to see him. Her parents weren't the only tempestuous ones in the bunch. When Mercedes and Quinn first met, when she auditioned for a spot as a backup singer in his rock band, they had their rocky moments. Diego and Tamara reconciled after a stormy breakup, having to deal with his pride and her strong-willed nature.

And she and Suave had certainly had words, as well, in the beginning. Their differences seemed trivial the more attached she grew to him. Differences of opinion and attitude were normal. What mattered was the bond and mutual respect and—most of all—the love that kept them together. She could see all of these growing more and more.

Alina walked behind Tamara in the hallway toward the door, both carrying boxes. Then Ellie Rivera walked through the front door that her father had left open—which meant that Suave couldn't be far behind.

She saw Tamara and grinned from ear to ear. "Hi, Tamara!"

"Hi, baby! Good to see you!" She bent to receive a kiss on the cheek.

"Hey, honey, thanks for coming!" Alina also tilted to the side, awaiting her hello kiss.

Ellie's smile faded, and she coldly slipped past Alina. "Hi, Alina."

Alina's first reaction was hurt, but then she pushed it away. Ellie was a kid; as a mother, Alina knew kids could be quirky sometimes, especially when they'd been awakened too early and hurried out of the house.

The real drama was taking place outside. The moving van's rear door was open, and a sour-faced Quinn stood on the platform, his hands on his waist. Diego sat on the ramp, biting on a knuckle and watching Alejandro and Carmela going at it, the new topic of discussion being the placement of items in the truck. Mercedes sat on the curb with Justin, both with their chins in their hands, looking frustrated.

And then there was Suave, walking up to them from his car. He tucked his car keys into his pocket and glanced to the side, catching sight of Alina.

What a smile. His eyes smiled with his mouth, the effect both sweet and provocative.

Alejandro walked to the other side of the truck with Carmela at his heels. Sighing, Tamara lowered a box onto the ground and addressed Diego. "So, what's the problem now?"

"Uh, your father feels that Quinn and I should pack the heaviest stuff in first. Then the boxes, not mixed together. Quinn and I would just like to get this done before the next Ice Age. And your mother is telling your father, basically, 'So, who's trying to tell the *muchachos* what to do *now?*' "

Ellie popped back out of the house and trotted down the walk toward the adults. "Is there anything you guys—"

Suave wrapped an arm around Alina, planting a quick greeting kiss on her lips. Out of the corner of her eye, she saw Ellie frown at her.

"—want me to carry?" The little girl plopped down on the curb beside Justin.

"Don't worry, pumpkin, we got work for you," Quinn promised her with a thumbs-up. Then he nodded at Tamara. "So, are you going to send your parents to their room, or should I? It's not my place to do it, but I'm *this* close."

Tamara faced her younger sister. "Mercedes, I thought you were showing Mami the truck to entertain her."

"Yes, but it's a truck, not an art exhibit! How entertained do you want her to be?"

With her sisters starting to snap at each other, Alina took control of the situation.

"No, I like Quinn's idea better. And it *is* my place to do it. I'll do it gently, respectfully, but firmly." She stepped around the truck and sang out, "Mami! Papi! Can you come here, please?"

Behind her, she heard Justin telling Ellie, "Mami's going to give Abuelo and Abuela time-out. *Cool!*"

Ellie's resentful retort caused Alina's heart to

sink. "If she does, I hope they give *her* a time-out."

"Justin, it's been a long day, honey. Why don't we call it a night? Justin?"

Alina took a cup of tea with her into the living room, where her son was curled up like a sleeping kitten on the couch. The television was still on, and all around Justin, the room looked like a warehouse, with piles of boxes scattered here and there. However daunting it looked, she resigned herself to the fact that it would look like that for a while as she found new homes for their belongings.

She set her cup down on the coffee table, switched off the TV, and scooped Justin up in her arms. Her big boy was getting bigger, taking after his father. He nestled his head against her neck as she carried him up the stairs.

His voice was sweet and groggy in her ear. "I'm sleeping in my room?"

"Yep. You have your own room again. Isn't that nice?"

"I like that." He lifted his head to look at her. "And where are you sleeping, Mami?"

"Right next door to you, honey. Not far away at all."

Earlier in the evening, she feared he'd be too wired to sleep. It hadn't taken that long to move, but then she had to return the truck, accompanied by Suave. Her sisters, brothers-in-law, Suave, and Ellie joined her for dinner at a local Chinese restaurant, and then, one by one, everyone went home.

It was a good day, all in all. Although it had begun with everyone getting on each other's nerves, and the afternoon's heat and humidity hadn't helped, it had turned out well in the end.

"This house makes lots of noises at night."

She tucked Justin into bed and cuddled up next to him.

"Old houses are like that," she said. "I don't know. I guess it's the wind going through the cracks. Like the house is getting comfortable before it falls asleep, too."

"Mami, how old is this house?"

"Oh, around seventy, maybe eighty years old, I think. She's an old lady, our house."

"She's older than Abuelo and Abuela?"

Alina chuckled. "Yeah, I believe she is. Although, those two aren't as old as you think they are. Well, you go to sleep. Mami's going to have her tea and then is going straight to bed, too." She pressed a soft kiss onto his cheek and rose.

"Mami, is Suave going to be my new daddy?" When she didn't answer right away, Justin sat up against his pillow. "If you and Suave get married, will I be his son?"

The question sobered the drowsiness right out of her. She returned to sit on the bed beside him, pushing straight, brown locks away from his forehead. She studied his expression carefully.

"If we got married, yes. He would . . . he would be like a second daddy to you. Why, honey? How would you feel about that?"

"Nice. I feel nice. I want a daddy."

Alina smiled, slowly. "I'm sure you do, honey."

"Suave would be a good daddy. He's nice to me."

"Well, if a man wasn't nice to you, I wouldn't even think about marrying him. But, I think you're right. Suave would be a good choice. And he's already a good daddy."

Justin's brow furrowed. "So, if you and him get married, does that make Ellie my sister?"

"That's the way it would work, yes. She'd be your stepsister." She was amused by his deepening frown. "Hmmm. Not a good idea, huh? What's the matter? Don't you like Ellie?"

"No!" Justin shook his head and covered his face with both tiny hands in a fit of dramatics.

"How come? She's nice to you."

"Yes, but she's mean to you."

Ah. You're a perceptive, little machito, *aren't you?* How would she explain this to a preschooler?

"Ellie lost her mommy, Justin. In the morning, we'll talk about this a lot more, I promise, but I want you to understand that Ellie's not mean. She just hurts a lot, in here." She patted the left side of his chest. "And she sees you and me—especially me—coming into her life and her daddy's, and she's scared. She's afraid she's going to lose her daddy."

"But why? I'll share you and him with her."

"Ay, Justin!" Alina really laughed that time. She leaned over and kissed him. "Give her time, that's all I'm saying. But Suave and I are not getting married right now. You, me, him, and Ellie—we all need time to get to know each other better. Okay?"

"Okay."

"All right, then. Goodnight, honey. I love you."

"Goodnight, Mami. I love you, too. And . . . you know what Abuela said?"

Alina stood at the door, holding it open. "What did Abuela say?" Her voice had a warning tone to it.

"She said that Papi—my real daddy, in heaven—is with me all the time. He watches over me. Is that true?"

She softened at the hopeful look in his eyes. "I believe that's true, yes."

"Even though I don't remember him? He still watches over me?"

"Oh, honey. You may not remember him, but I'm sure that, even in heaven, he remembers you." Alina blew him a kiss. "Now, you go to sleep, my little sweetheart."

And Ellie's mother probably watches over her. How I'd love to ask her how to get her little girl to open up to me!

She went downstairs and put her tea into the microwave for a few seconds. Justin had exaggerated Ellie's behavior that day. She had been frosty—rather than outright mean—toward Alina. For most of the day, Ellie had avoided contact with her, and she'd sulked when she saw her father sit beside Alina in the restaurant.

The green-eyed monster of jealousy had really turned that little girl's head. It would've been cute had Alina not felt so shut out by Ellie, unable to make some friendly gesture toward her. She took her tea and her cell phone up to bed with her, no longer able to stand, yearning to crash into bed.

She'd taken the cool treatment from Ellie in stride, even when she had called to her in the restaurant's parking lot to watch out for a car—and Ellie deliberately ignored her. Luckily, the car swerved out of the way in time—but the close call gave everyone a good scare, including Suave. That was when he took Ellie aside and, keeping his voice down, gave her a stern reprimand.

Alina drank half of her tea before turning off the lamp on her nightstand. To Ellie, she was the "other woman." She couldn't force the issue, either, by pushing herself into the little girl's life. She was waiting instead to be gradually accepted.

And it would happen, with patience and time. In the meantime, Alina felt sorry for both of them. For Ellie, who was at an age when she most needed a mother in her life, and for Suave, who was caught between a rock and a hard place.

With patience and time. For now, she surrendered to exhaustion and fell into a restful sleep.

Alina was a light sleeper, so she easily heard the cell phone ringing beside her bed. She jumped up, becoming aware of the morning light flooding through the bedroom window.

"Alina?" Suave said on the other line. "Oh, I'm sorry—you're still asleep."

"Oh, no, I'm up." She propped the pillows up behind her, smiling into the phone. It was a particularly pleasant experience, waking up to that voice. "Or I should be up, anyway, by now. I must've overslept."

"Uh-huh. It was all that running around yesterday."

He was going for a casual tone, yet she heard a tense edge to his voice. "Is everything okay, Suave."

"Well, that's—that's why I was calling you. I've already called the police, but I'm sitting here, waiting for them to come, and I had to do something, so—I wanted to hear your voice."

"The police?" Alina sat up fully. "What happened?"

There was a terrible pause on the other end. "Ellie ran away from home."

"She . . . no, she probably just went out for a walk or something. Maybe she went to—"

"Alina, she left me a good-bye note." She heard his ragged breathing. "She ran away, all right. My little girl's gone."

Ten

Dear Daddy,

I'm writing you this letter to say good-bye. By the time you get up I won't be here. I'm going to miss you but it's better that I leave.

Thank you for taking care of me since I was a baby. You always made me feel like I was really your kid. I'll miss you but I'll be okay. Please don't worry about me. Maybe I'll see you again someday.

I love you 4-Ever.

Love,
Ellie

Suave read the note again—he'd lost track of how many times—over the police officer's shoulder. He swallowed hard, feeling the back of his throat dry and scratchy.

"She's not your natural daughter, sir?" a female cop asked.

"No. I legally adopted Ellie when I married her mother. And she knows about it. We told her when she was eight or so, I think."

The male officer studied a recent picture, taken when they'd first moved to New Jersey from Las Vegas. His partner jotted notes in a pad, occasionally speaking into a radio attached to her shoulder. Suave glanced over at Alina sitting at the table with Justin on her lap.

"Any idea where she might've gone? You know, sometimes kids don't get very far. To a friend's house, maybe their grandmother's."

"My wife's family isn't from the area, and neither is mine. We moved here not too long ago, and I already checked with her friends' parents in the neighborhood."

"You know if maybe she has some money on her?"

"I give her an allowance. Ten dollars a week. She has a piggy bank, too, which she saves change in. But."—he sat down—"It was empty this morning when I checked."

The female cop took the picture and clipped it to her notebook. "Does she have any favorite places she likes to go to?"

"I really don't give Ellie that much free reign. She's only eleven and . . . she's a girl. She's allowed up and down the block with her friends, but I don't allow her to go that far without me or another adult, like one of the kids' parents."

"All right." The male cop cleared his throat. "We got enough to go on for now, with the missing person report. We're putting out an APB, getting her into the NCIC computer. Somebody should be here"—he jerked his head at Alina—

"in case she comes back, or she calls, anything. Let us know if she does. We'll drive around the area, look for her, and you'll hear from us if we do find her."

If. To Suave, at that moment, that word had never sounded so ominous.

He walked the cops to the door, thanking them on their way out. His motions felt mechanical and unnatural, from the moment he'd first found Ellie's note on the kitchen table. Not only was all of her change missing—about nine dollars—but some of her clothes, her backpack, her portable CD player, and a favorite stuffed animal were also gone.

Because Ellie ran away from home. He told himself that over and over, and it still made no sense. She'd never done that before—and God knows he'd never done it, as a kid, or his father would've tarred the roof with him. Ellie, all fifty pounds of her, was somewhere out there, yet he didn't know where. If she'd used her change to board a bus, there was no telling where she could be. He remembered how fond she was of Manhattan from the few times they'd traveled out to the city, and the very thought was horrifying.

That, alone, was dangerous thinking. Crime and predators were everywhere, not restricted to New York City. He walked back to the kitchen to get his keys from the bowl on top of the refrigerator.

"You'll stay here, Alina?" he asked. "I'm going out, too, see if I find her. I shouldn't be too long."

"Of course. Take this with you, Suavecito." She

removed her cell phone from her purse and handed it to him. "If she comes home, I'll call you right away."

Holding the toy dog that Suave had given him in the hospital, Justin looked up at him. Justin had silently watched the police with wide, brown eyes filled with curiosity, realizing something was terribly wrong. His smile was hesitant as he held up the stuffed animal, bobbing his head up and down.

"Ellie coming back, Suave," Justin said, providing a funny voice for the dog. "She'll come home."

Suave patted the dog and ruffled Justin's hair. "Thanks, buddy. And thanks to you, too, little man."

"You wait right here, honey. I'll be right back. Just walking Suave to the door," Alina said.

"I have to go out and look for her myself. I have to do something." He walked ahead of her in the apartment's short hallway. "Or maybe I should stay here, I don't know. You probably have something else to do today, Alina. I don't want to impose upon you."

"It's no imposition, Suave. Those boxes are going to be there for a while. I can stay, but I think you have to keep your head straight. Let the police do their job."

"I can't. I can't stand around, not doing anything. It feels worse." He unlocked the door and opened it. "Especially because I brought this on myself. I snapped at her a couple times yesterday, she was being such a nudge. That's not like her."

Alina let her eyes drop to his chest. Her normally pretty face was lined with concern.

"I don't think you're the cause of this happening." She sounded so crestfallen. "We can talk about that later. You go."

"Hey, Alina. . . ."

She looked up, and he cupped her face, bringing her chin up.

"This has nothing to do with you," he said, firmly.

"She never did anything like this before I came into the picture, either. Maybe she's not ready, and maybe we shouldn't push things—"

"Alina, Alina, I have to go. Please don't go thinking that way while I'm gone."

He got into his car, pulled out, and turned the corner, not really sure of where to go. Suave felt ill. He'd had nothing to eat or drink, not even his usual morning coffee.

She will come back. She has to. Ellie was upset over the attention he'd been giving Alina, angry because he'd scolded and punished her for her rudeness. Surely, she was somewhere nearby, hoping in that preteen way to teach her father a lesson by scaring him. Before noon, he'd be calling the police to inform them she was home, safe and sound.

And what if noon comes and goes, and she's still not back? What if she doesn't come home at all? He should have talked to her. He tried to before he left for that weekend. Why didn't he see the warning signals?

And what was going to happen to her, his

Ellie, if she never came home at all? It was funny, how many of those pictures he'd seen on milk cartons and on public-service announcements on television, pictures of other people's children, never once considering that could be his child.

His *adopted* child. It didn't matter that he loved her as his own flesh and blood. It was how *she* saw their relationship.

You always made me feel like I was really your kid. Did she really think him that noble, that he would spend his life doing her a favor? To him, she *was* really his child. He remembered an adage he'd read somewhere about how if every child in the world were tossed up in the air and landed in one big pile, every parent would still pick out his own. Never mind the brightest or the prettiest or the best behaved—your own would be your pick.

He would have made a beeline through that crowd and picked Ellie. She may have had another man's eyes, but she had Suave's heart.

After turning off Main Street, he parked by a card store Ellie often frequented to buy her favorite candy bars and, if she had the money, the latest Beanie Baby to add to her collection. He caught his breath.

This was surreal, worse than a nightmare. That was as far as he could go without covering his eyes with one hand as the desperate tears fought their way down his face.

* * *

Noon came and went. So did the rest of the afternoon as the day aged into early evening. Alina sat in Suave's living room, her shoes kicked off and her feet crossed at the ankles on the coffee table. From there, she could see Tamara closing the door to Ellie's bedroom.

"Well, Justin went off for a nap," her sister said. "Can't let him sleep too long, or he won't be sleepy by his regular bedtime."

"How well you know that child."

Tamara sank into the couch cushions. "In a little bit, I'll make some dinner. I don't know if anybody's hungry, but I don't think it helps any to not eat."

"Make something light. Nothing that's too much trouble. We can warm it up for Suave when he gets back."

"That's what I was thinking, too." Tamara grabbed one of the throw pillows, clutching it to her lap. "So you only have a few days before you start work in the new school. You're looking forward to it?"

Alina found it interesting how she and her sister had made small talk for part of the day. It was human nature to strive for some normalcy, for that calm center within the storm. It was hard not to notice the storm, too, with Suave in and out of the apartment all day, leaving periodically to drive around the area. He returned each time more quiet and forlorn than he'd left.

"You're asking me if I'm glad my long summer vacation is over," she quipped.

"True. You know, I always wondered if that's why you became a teacher. You just didn't want to give up that little perk of being a kid."

Tamara laughed with her. Her sister had arrived that afternoon, providing Alina with some company and Suave with the support of a longtime friend. She'd watched Justin for an hour when Alina accompanied him on one of the drives. They'd returned to find Tamara lying on the carpet with him, each with a coloring book and crayons.

"You think you're so smart, don't you? For your information, I did it for that other perk."

"Which is?"

"A brand-new wardrobe every September." Alina laughed again. "Only it hasn't always worked that way. Now with this mortgage, it's certainly *not* going to work that way."

"My favorite part about going back to school was getting to go to the games again," Tamara mused. "Not just basketball, either. All of the games. I used to love just being in the stadium or at the court."

"Nope. For me, it was the clothes. That big shopping spree Mami took us on about a week before school. Definitely, the clothes!"

Tamara bumped against her, the sisterly version of roughhousing. "Yeah, you were so superficial back then. When did you become human? You didn't notify me before you did it."

The cordless telephone rang on the coffee table in front of them. The two sisters silently stared at it. At the second ring, Alina reached for it.

"Hello?"

"Hello? Is my daddy there?"

She tightened her hold on Tamara's arm and sat up. "Ellie? Where are you, honey?"

"I'm in Horizon Beach."

Alina motioned to Tamara, who ran into the kitchen to find a pad and pen.

"Where in Horizon Beach are you right now?"

"I'm on the boardwalk. I was in New York before, but I came back."

"You were in New York?" Then she erased the alarm from her voice, speaking calmly. "But you're back here now, right?"

"Uh-huh."

"And where on the boardwalk are you?"

"I'm not really on the boardwalk, I'm like—I'm near it. You come down the ramp, and there's Milt's Arcade, and there's a phone. . . ."

"Okay, okay, I think I know where that is." Alina saw Tamara run back into the room, and she took the pen and a sheet of notebook paper from her. "The first thing you see when you walk up the ramp, on the left, that's the fortune teller, isn't it?"

"Hold on. Let me look." A moment passed while she heard the phone being moved around. "That's Madame Ophelia's?"

"Yes, that's it. I know where you are. Ellie, are you all right?"

"Yes. But it's getting dark. And I'm tired. And I don't have any money left." Her voice broke into a sob. "I want my daddy to come and get me. Or can you come? I wanna come home now."

Alina's heart broke listening to Ellie cry on the other end. "Oh, honey, I'm getting in touch with your daddy right now, as soon as I get off the phone with you. Ellie, listen to me. Right across from the fortune teller, there's a restaurant. Tell them that you're waiting there for your dad to pick you up, and you wait there, until he comes. Okay?"

"Okay. Tell him to hurry, Alina."

"Oh, he will. You wait there." She hung up the phone and then immediately punched in her cell phone number. "She's on the boardwalk in Horizon Beach."

Tamara exhaled in relief. "That's the next town over. Wouldn't the cops have—"

"She went to New York first, then turned around and came back."

"New York!"

"Let's just be grateful she turned back!" Tucking her legs under her and putting the phone back to her ear, she felt jubilant.

The phone rang three times before Suave answered. "Alina?"

"Hi. Get over to the boardwalk in Horizon Beach. She's near the amusement pier, sitting in the restaurant across from the fortune teller."

"She called? She's all right?"

The joy in his voice brought a smile to her. "Yes, she's all right. She's sitting in there, waiting for you."

"Alina, I'm a couple towns over from Horizon

Beach. Can you get there first and meet me, baby?"

She hadn't expected that sweet invitation. It was intimate and familial, coming with a potent burst of love.

"For you and Ellie? I'm on my way."

Eleven

Jim's Seaside Palace was a favorite of Justin's. It was built to resemble a railroad dining car, and the main entrees on its menus were painted above the wide windows: BUTTERMILK PANCAKES, CHICKEN IN THE BASKET, ALL THE SHRIMP YOU CAN EAT. For the summer, if at no other time during the year, the Jim with no last name had himself a mint. Alina had never seen the place empty.

The locals and out-of-town party animals were beginning to filter onto the boardwalk, which was a loud collection of noise and multicolored lights. If they weren't there for the amusement pier, with its rides, game booths, and other attractions, the people were killing time until the bars opened. Parking anywhere near the boardwalk was virtually nonexistent. Alina saved herself time by parking at home and walking the three blocks to the beach.

As she walked up the boardwalk ramp, she spotted Ellie in the one of the restaurant's windows. She looked tiny and lost in a big booth by herself. Her long, sandy-brown hair was in disarray, the strands wildly straying from the ponytail holder.

She nibbled on something, stopping to sip through a straw.

There was no denying that she was Tracy Alredge's child. It took looking at the small-scale version for Alina to realize how pretty the original had been. With one detectable difference: She couldn't remember that same innocence in Tracy's face, which made her little girl all the more precious.

Ellie looked up and saw Alina's gaze meeting hers through the glass. Perhaps because she saw a familiar face, the light came back into the little girl's eyes and she jumped out of the booth.

Alina hastened through the door, stunned to have her arms filled with Ellie a moment later. She comforted her with a tight hug, rubbing her back gently.

"I am so glad to see you!" Alina didn't hold back her excitement.

"Me, too!" Shyly, Ellie freed herself from the embrace. "Where's my dad?"

"He's on his way. He was out looking for you when you called. Why don't we sit down and wait for him?"

In the booth, on Ellie's side of the table, was Justin's favorite dish, chicken in the basket. There was one well-nibbled drumstick, and most of the cheese fries and Pepsi were gone.

"So, how's my girl doing? Is this a friend of yours, Ellie?"

Alina looked up into the face of a pudgy, bleached-blond woman in a pink-and-blue waitress uniform. She sounded friendly enough for

Ellie's sake, but she regarded Alina in a suspicious way.

"Um, she's my dad's girlfriend," Ellie responded.

"Oh. Okay. So you know her, then." The waitress smiled at Alina then and pulled a check pad from her pocket. "Can I get you something, Miss? A menu? Coffee?"

"Uh, no, thank you. We're just waiting for her dad."

"Daddy's on his way. Good." The woman patted Ellie's arm. "And how's your chicken, sweetie? You're enjoying it?"

"Yep. It's really good. Thank you."

"You're very welcome, honey."

"Well, at least you're eating a good meal," Alina told Ellie as soon as the waitress left them alone.

"I told her I didn't have any money, but she brought it for me, anyway. She said it was 'on the house.' "

"Oh. Did you tell her you were waiting for us?"

"Uh-huh. And she saw me outside, talking on the phone to you. She said I could sit here as long as I wanted."

"Ah, I see."

And the waitress had probably seen Ellie red-eyed from crying when she'd walked into the restaurant. That also explained her checking Alina out, making sure she wasn't a stranger. She smiled at a woman who tended a young family of three at another table, and returned her attention to Ellie.

"There are some nice people in this world, like

her. And there are some who are not so nice, Ellie. I hope you didn't meet up with any of them today."

"I didn't." She played with her straw. "I know I'm close to home, but I didn't know how to get back. I used up all my money."

"Oh? On the bus ride to New York and back?"

"And on lunch. And the rides on the board-walk." Losing interest in her meal, Ellie tossed a half-eaten cheese fry onto her plate. "It's no fun, you know. Going to the amusement pier by your-self."

"No, I'd think not. You know what it is? These places aren't made to go to by yourself. They were made with friends and family in mind."

Alina didn't go further with the issue. She didn't want it to sound like she was scolding Ellie. Ellie took no offense, offering a weary smile.

"Did my dad tell you to come for me?"

"He asked me to meet him here. He thought I'd get here sooner, which I did, and he didn't want you alone too long, waiting for him."

"Is he mad at me? He must be so mad at me. This was so stupid—"

"He's not mad at you, Ellie. He was just scared. Your dad was afraid he'd never see you again."

Ellie tried to control her lower lip, which couldn't stop trembling. Embarrassed, she looked away from Alina and stared out the window.

"Me, too. That's why I wanted to come back, be-cause I thought I would never see him again. But I thought that's what he wanted."

Alina saw the rest of her beginning to shake.

Ellie was trying so hard to be a big girl and not cry as fiercely as she had on the phone. Alina wanted nothing more than to scoot over to the her side of that booth and comfort her, but she restrained herself.

"Why would you *ever* think that about your dad, Ellie?"

"Um . . . because"—she dabbed a napkin at her nose—"I don't know if he told you, but he's not my real father. My real dad left my mom and me."

"He did? Well, he threw away something very important. Because you're a great kid, and from what I remember, your mom was a great lady."

"She was." Wiping her face with the back of her hands, Ellie blinked at her. "You knew my mom?"

"I sure did. Oh—not very well, you know. She was a little younger than me, closer to your dad's age. In fact, I was just thinking to myself, when I saw you in here, how much you look like her. And it made me smile, because she was pretty as a picture, too."

Ellie nodded. She said hoarsely, "I miss her a lot."

"I'm sure you do, honey. That's natural. I'm a grown-up, and I know that whenever it comes time for my mother to pass away, I'll miss her so much, too. Your mother is your mother. And the truth is"—she folded her hands on the table, speaking kindly to her—"no one will ever replace her in your heart. They can't."

At that, her voice broke. Across the table, Ellie wiped away a tear rolling down her nose. Alina sniffed and sat back.

"But you're not alone. You know that, right?" She continued in a more upbeat tone. "Because you have a father who loves you very, very much. He was probably the father that you were supposed to have, and he found his way to you. You know what he told me?"

Inching her way forward, Ellie asked, "What?"

"He was telling me about the day you were born. His whole face changes when he tells that story." She laughed. "You can tell he's talking about the most wonderful day of his life. Does that sound like someone who, all of a sudden, doesn't have room in his life for you?"

Ellie didn't trust herself to speak and replied with a shake of her head.

"And I know that you love him. There's a big part of your heart that belongs to your mother, and a big part that belongs to your dad. As for me"—Alina moved forward again—"I would be happy with just a very little part of your heart. Really tiny. I promise—I'll take very good care of it."

The girl giggled with her and pushed hair from her face. "I'm sorry I was mean to you, Alina."

"It's forgotten. Let's just start fresh, okay?" She extended her hand across the table, pleased to have it clutched by a smaller one. "Friends?"

"Friends."

"Good. Now look out the window and see who's there."

"Daddy?" Ellie looked to her right and gasped. *"Daddy!"*

She nearly knocked over her glass in her haste to run out of the restaurant, making Alina laugh heartily. Ellie forgot her backpack, too. Grabbing it by a strap, Alina rose and watched the reunion through the window, respecting the private moment between father and daughter, something she was well familiar with.

Suave had only taken a couple of steps off the ramp before he saw Ellie running toward him. He'd been put through the mill that day, exhausted from driving and searching and fretting. Even with windblown hair and faded jeans over his long, muscular legs, he looked incredibly handsome. He'd perfected a fatherly smile, too, with all its tenderness. He stretched his arms to catch Ellie and sweep her up. Alina's heart beat faster and she wished she could preserve the moment forever.

She felt someone beside her and heard a deep, female voice say, "And *that* must be Daddy!"

Alina grinned at the waitress. "How did you ever guess?"

"Just a hunch." The woman winked at her. "Have a good night, Miss."

"You, too. And thank you for everything."

She joined Suave and Ellie on the boardwalk, where amused onlookers chuckled at the over six-foot-tall man having his face covered by an eleven-year-old's kisses. He set her down and held her face in his hands.

"Don't you *ever* do that again, Ellie, please," he whispered loudly. "Don't you *ever* scare me like that again. I love you too much."

"No, never. I love you, too."

Suave hugged her, looking over her head at Alina, who stood close by. He smiled and motioned with his arm, forming a circle with the two most important women in his life. Alina rose on tiptoe so that she could kiss him.

"We're going to talk when we get home," he told Ellie. "We have a lot of talking to do. And I'm not the only one that's going to be talking, either."

"Okay."

"Tonight, or tomorrow, if you're tired. But we're gonna clear the air, have no more misunderstandings. The first thing I have to know is . . . did you spend the whole day at the boardwalk?"

Ellie laughed along with Alina. Feeling outnumbered by the two women, Suave pleaded his case with the adult one, "No, I'm serious. I combed this place a couple of times. You'd think the cops would've looked here, too—"

"Suavecito, I don't think you really want to know where she was. Does he, Ellie?" She thought the girl's furious shake of her head humorous. "No, you'll be in more trouble, then!"

"Oh, it can't be that bad. It's not like she went to New York or anything!"

Both Ellie and Alina dropped their heads, exchanging glances like confidantes. It had been a hard enough day, so he chose not to ask.

"You know, it'll be one of those things, Daddy," Ellie defended herself sweetly, "that we'll laugh at, years and years to come."

"Yeah, you better hope so!" He hugged her

again, shooting a mock-stern look at Alina. "And that goes for *both* of you!"

"I think running away lost its mystique pretty quickly," Alina said. "So, she came here for the rides, but she found they weren't as much fun when you go on them by yourself."

"No, they never are. Even after everything you put me through today, young lady, I'll let you have one ride before we go home. *One*. But I know you, Ellie. You're going to pick the roller coaster, and I'm too wiped out to get thrown around."

"That's okay, Daddy. I know you're tired."

Slowly glancing to her left at the woman she'd once seen as her arch rival and seeing her in another light, Ellie brightened.

"Would you ride the roller coaster with me, Alina?"

The invitation came with a warm hand on her arm, containing a mild tug. Alina accepted it for what it was: a touching olive leaf, and a beginning.

"Oh, baby. I thought you'd never ask!"

Around eleven o'clock, nature provided its own cooling system. The day's heat and humidity resulted in a storm, backed by the power and fervor of summer coming to an end.

The enclosed porch provided a safe theater to observe the torrent. Suave sat in one of two rattan rockers, drowsily admiring the show. Lightning whipped a path across the sky above the houses on the opposite side of the street, seconds before thunder struck, loud and awesome. The rain sounded like percussion following its own rhythm against the windows.

How he loved storms...from a distance. Suave stretched his legs and groaned contentedly. As soon as he hit the bed, he'd be out like a light. It was hard to believe that a day that had begun so badly could transform into a masterpiece by its end.

The screen door rattled open, and Alina stepped onto the porch. She sat in the other rocker and released a huge, deep sigh.

"Yeah, my sentiments exactly," Suave teased. "Are they both asleep?"

"Finally. Justin was the hard one tonight. I never thought I'd get that little jumping bean in bed. Ellie went right to sleep."

"Well, giving your father a heart attack takes a lot out of you. I can't tell you what it feels like to have her back."

"*My* sentiments, exactly. Neither can I."

He shifted in his chair to face her. Her hair fell loosely over one shoulder, prompting him to touch it.

"It wasn't your fault, you know. It was mine. I should've realized how upset she was, and then I had to go and scold her and everything—"

"And you did right. A parent who loves has to discipline, or he doesn't love enough." She was straightforward with him. "But, Suave, you *know* I had something to do with it."

"What I *know* is that you said something to her

tonight that touched her. Whatever it was, Ellie saw you in a different light. And I know it'll take time. It's not going to be overnight—but Alina, I believe she could become very attached to you."

"Really?" She said hopefully.

"Yeah. Really. Take it from me. It's very hard *not* to get attached to you."

The light from one lightning bolt miles away instantly lit up the porch. They watched through the window in hopes of catching another one. Suave's hand sought hers on the arm of her chair, and they both rocked gently.

Alina couldn't remember ever having been so enthralled by a storm. The night had made up for the day with a natural display of fireworks. Tamara had cooked dinner and went home after eating with them, and then they'd spent time with the children until bedtime. During the last portion of the night, they'd stolen a few moments for themselves, relaxing in each other's company.

She faced him again. "I already feel so attached to you, too, Suave."

He pushed his glasses back further on his nose. "Just attached?"

"No, a lot more than that. I've known you for so long, but it's like when you came back into my life, you brought me a happiness that hasn't been there in a long time."

Suave reached behind her, pulling her closer across the arms of their chairs. He had a physical need to kiss her that had been there all night, prevented by the children and Tamara and the steady flow of activity. She silently conveyed how much she wanted his kiss, prolonging it and responding with another, hungrier one.

Two bolts flashed rapidly, lighting the porch again, and then it softly dimmed again. The lightning and thunder might as well have been trapped inside them for all the emotion that flowed from his body to hers.

In the heat of the moment, he confessed. "I thought, today, that you were going to tell me you didn't want us to be together because of what happened."

Alina brushed her hand across his cheek. "And I thought you were going to have second thoughts about us. That maybe Ellie wasn't ready. I just wanted to accept whatever you thought was best, even though what I really want is to be with you."

"Oh." Suave chuckled. "We can love our kids, but we can't live our lives for them, Alina. Especially because I know how good it would for Ellie to have you in her life. It's already done me a lot of good, loving you."

She kissed him again, so joyous she laughed. "It's not an easy thing. It's two families. It's your family, and it's my family, and if—if this was to develop more, it would be of matter of two families becoming one."

"No, not an easy thing at all. And it would begin with you and me making a life together."

The rain beat harder against the windows. Together with the howl of the wind and the rumble of distant thunder, the sounds formed a majestic symphony that filled the peaceful silence between them.

It was perfect weather for Alina to curl up beside Suave and rest in his arms. She brought her gaze from the windows to his face, filled with an encompassing love for him.

"You and I could make a life together," she said confidently. "And *what* a life we would make together."

Epilogue

Halfway through the meal, Alejandro Romero—older and grayer, perhaps, but just as distinguished as always—rose from his seat at the head of the table with a glass of red wine in his hand.

"I did not forget that we need to toast our guest of honor," he said, looking at Ellie.

Alina set down her fork to look at her stepdaughter, who was sitting between her and Suave. Looking around the table, she saw the rest of her family doing the same, with silverware clinking against dishes and glasses being raised.

Her parents could not have possibly fit another person at that table if they'd tried. It was the same table that, for thousands of dinners gone by, had accommodated a family of five. It now seated the host and hostess, their three daughters, three sons-in-law, and Ellie—who at seventeen had outgrown the smaller table set for the children. Having just turned ten that month, Justin had balked at the injustice of the seating arrangements. His grandfather had informed him with amusement that those were the breaks. He'd be joining his sister at the "big" table soon enough.

Too soon. Alina took her own glass, acknowledging her father, and one of her closest friends, with a nod.

"Ellie, this celebration is in your honor," Alejandro began. "And this toast is especially for you, because next week, you are going to Virginia to the college where your future is going to begin, and we are all very proud of you."

He stopped to catch his breath, putting a hand over the left side of his chest. Diego Santamaria was never one to let an opportunity to tease his father-in-law pass him, and he raised a hand into the air.

"You sure you're going to get through this toast?" he asked.

"I think so. If I need your help, I'll yell." Alejandro laughed with satisfaction and returned to his toast. "You all have to be patient with me, because to me, this is emotional. It's been a long time since I saw one daughter go to college—"

Alina beamed when he looked at her.

"—and then, another daughter left my house for her future—"

That smile was for Tamara, waving back at him from beside Diego, who wrapped an arm around her.

"—and a *third* daughter, who told me she didn't want to go to college, because she wanted to become *an actress!*"

Mercedes pretended to be very interested in the rim of her wineglass but shared a humorous glance with her father.

"And she did. And besides becoming an actress, she joined a rock-and-roll band and gave me a fine son-in-law, who also happened to be the lead singer. I am old enough to know that these things have a way of working out for the best." He waited for the laughter to subside and added, "And she's happy, and that's all that I care about. But now. . . ."

Alejandro turned back to Ellie, who gazed at him with deep affection and love.

"It is *your* turn, Ellie, to follow your dreams." Raising his glass higher, he gave the toast. "You take with you the love and the encouragement of all of us, your family. You leave here a young woman with aspirations, and you will return, knowing how to achieve them. And every one sitting here believes, with all their heart, that you will. To Ellie—*salud!*"

As glasses around the table clinked, Alina paid special attention to the young lady she'd raised as her own daughter. Ellie basked in being the star of the moment, clinking her glass of Pepsi with the adults' wineglasses. And Alina felt that little sadness, the empty-nest syndrome that would occur again when Justin grew into a young man.

Ellie turned to hug her father, kissing him and telling him she loved him. It was still adorable to watch them together—tall Suave and his petite, slender daughter. She'd become a young woman before their eyes, beautiful and poised.

"Alina, I love you so much."

She was ready for her own kiss and enthusiastic hug. "I love you, too, honey. Very much."

Leaning forward to look past the other adults, Ellie smiled at Alejandro. "Thank you, Abuelo."

He offered her a regal bow of his head. "It's true, *mi cielito.*"

Quinn rested his arm on the back of Mercedes' chair and changed the subject.

"Alejandro, let me ask you a question, although I'm sure other people have asked you this. As the father of three daughters, did you ever wish for a son?"

"Well, you are right. I have been asked that. So I will answer it again." The Romero patriarch was making it clear that he enjoyed the limelight.

Carmela leaned closer to Suave, telling him in a loud whisper, "Oh, he *loves* to tell this story!"

Alejandro listened to everyone laugh and shook a finger at his wife. "And you love to hear me tell it. Be honest! Anyway, when my first daughter was about to be born, I was convinced that it was going to be a boy. I told everyone we're having a son! And, ah—there was Alina."

He didn't rush the pause, sharing a long, affectionate gaze with Alina.

"And then the second time, I was certain—well, this one, *this one,*" he pounded his fist lightly on the table, amusing his audience. "This one is the boy! We get down to the hospital, the baby is born, and—hello, Tamara!"

"Oh, come on!" Diego tossed back at him. "I'm glad you had a girl! This one's mine!"

Alejandro nodded back at him. "Then, the

third time of going down to the hospital, I am *positive* that lightning could not possibly strike three times! I had two beautiful daughters that I would not trade for an army of sons, but *oye*—if you give me a son, I'm going to take him. So we bring home—a girl named Mercedes!"

Suave wrapped up the story for him, telling him through a smile, "So, you didn't have sons. You had three adventures that made you and Carmela very proud, in the form of three daughters."

Glaring at him, the older gentleman motioned to his wife. "Do you hear your son-in-law? He is not allowed to tell the ending. That's the best part!"

"Ah, Alejandro—you'll live!" Carmela's sauciness won her applause and a playful wink from her husband. She rose, collecting a few of the dishes and silverware. "Let us clean up a little bit, and we can relax and have dessert and coffee."

"We'll do that, Mami," Alina offered.

"No, Alina, we have it. You and Suave relax." Mercedes told her. She took her husband by the arm as he rose. *"We,* as in *you* and *me,* mister!"

Quinn eyed her innocently. "Oh, I was—just about to do that!"

Ellie also moved around the table, collecting silverware, plates, and casserole dishes. Tamara left to start coffee brewing in the kitchen. Diego went to the children's table, bravely rolling up his sleeves to attack the mess left in their wake. The grandparents were banished from the dining room while the clean up took place, so instead they headed for the living room.

Alina felt a tug at her arm, and she twirled around to see Suave jerking his head toward the hallway. Because they'd only get in the way if they stayed in the living room, she allowed her husband to lead her to the foyer, the only private room on the first floor of the house.

He took her in his arms and kissed her fully on the mouth, this man who'd taken that second trip down the aisle with her, who'd claimed her heart as his own. It had taken six years to build their marriage upon mutual devotion, respect, and friendship, filled with true love.

Holding him, she looked up into his face and said, "This won't be private that long. Someone is bound to find us in here."

"That's okay. All I wanted was one little minute, just to tell you how much you mean to me," Suave told her emphatically. "And to thank you."

"Thank me for what?"

"For not letting me go to that cabin by myself."

"Suavecito, Suavecito. I would not have missed that for the world!" She raised a finger in the air. "Later. You and me, alone. *Later.* Right now, we have to go join them."

"Okay. Later, right?"

"Later, definitely."

Alina opened the door for them, taking him by the hand. "You know, baby, my dad is really in his glory now."

"Why's that?" Then, Suave laughed as they walked into the living room.

Alejandro was on the couch, wrestling with four young men: Justin; Diego and Tamara's six-year-old son, Manny; Quinn and Mercedes' five-year-old, Christopher; and the newest addition to Suave and Alina's family, four-year-old Sean.

The question had already been answered, but Alina couldn't resist.

"Just look at all those boys!"

COMING IN JULY 2001
FROM ENCANTO ROMANCE

__THE PERFECT MIX
by Caridad Scordato   0-7860-1276-5 $4.99US/6.99CAN

Streetwise and savvy, Blanca Martinez is leery of her enigmatic new contractor. Something tells her that he hasn't always been the polished craftsman he appears to be. As Rey transforms a rundown building into the restaurant of her dreams, Blanca is driven to uncover the truth about the man he once was—and irresistibly drawn to the man he has become . . .

__WINDOW TO PARADISE
by Erica Fuentes   0-7860-1181-5 $4.99US/$6.99CAN

Widowed single mom Valentina Vallardares is certain it's going to take more than an extended vacation on her godmother's Hawaiian ranch to heal her heartache. Warmly embraced by the fun-loving Saaverdra family, a reluctant Valentina is soon captivated by the exotic island—and by a certain carefree cowboy whose heated gaze unexpectedly stirs molten desire . . .

USE THE COUPON ON THE NEXT PAGE TO ORDER

New Romances From Encanto!